THE SUMMER THE SPIES MOVED IN

Other Apple Paperbacks
you will enjoy:

Glass Slippers Give You Blisters
by Mary Jane Arch

Marrying Off Mom
by Martha Tolles

The Kissing Contest
by Dian Curtis Regan

*I Spent My Summer Vacation
Kidnapped into Space*
by Martin Godfry

Home Sweet Home, Good-bye
by Cynthia Stowe

THE SUMMER THE SPIES MOVED IN

MARY LOCKE

AN
APPLE
PAPERBACK

SCHOLASTIC INC.
New York Toronto London Auckland Sydney

ISBN 0-590-43723-2

12 11 10 9 8 7 6 5 4   4 5 6/9

Printed in the U.S.A.   28

First Scholastic printing, June 1991

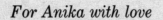

For Anika with love

1

The three emerged from the big blue car as though they already belonged in the neighborhood. The burly man unfolded himself slowly from the driver's seat and stood by the car, stretching and arching his back. His head seemed huge, with thick wavy hair; his face was dominated by eyebrows. A short, square woman with no neck hurried busily from the car to the front door, keys in hand.

Meg, on watch from her front stoop across the street, focused on the girl who had slid gracefully, long legs first, from the backseat. The girl wore a loose-fitting green dress topped with a wide-brimmed straw hat. She held onto her hat and took a couple of steps back to get a full view of the house. She said something that made the man laugh aloud.

Meg feigned indifference with a yawn and a stretch.

The girl, hands now on hips, began to survey

her surroundings. Her eyes traveled from one brick colonial house to the next, across spacious, well-tended lawns, over hedges and two white picket fences. It was a defiant survey, head held high, as though she didn't quite believe the singing birds, the splashes of colorful flowers, the alternating greens of the trees and grass. Finally, the girl's visual tour arrived at Meg's house.

Meg stopped mid-stretch. "Hey, I know that girl," she muttered to herself.

"Huh? What'd you say?" Dorie's voice and body burst through the screen door behind Meg.

Even the sound of the banging door could not rouse the interest of the girl across the street. She took no notice of Meg and Dorie, not a wave, not a smile, not even a frown. Instead, she kept turning her face, slowly and deliberately, taking time to study each remaining house in sight. Then she took the man's offered arm and, talking animatedly now, walked with him into the house.

It was mid-June, barely nine-thirty in the morning, and already the humidity had dampened Meg's T-shirt and shorts and tightened the brown curls that framed her face. Washington, D.C., was reaffirming its local reputation as The Swamp.

"That girl who just went in the house across the street — I saw her at the school carnival last month," Meg told Dorie as she leaned back on her elbows, pensive. "She won the prize I wanted."

"Who is she?" Dorie planted herself in front of

Meg, each high-top red sneaker in the center of a flagstone. Meg knew Dorie was avoiding the cracks.

"Somebody weird."

"How come?"

"See, I was standing in the Super Chance line for the third time. You know, it's the best booth, from a financial point of view, at the school carnival. Every ticket wins a prize."

Dorie put her hands on her hips, head tilted to one side. "I think the prizes are boring. Who wants pencils, erasers, paper hats? The PTA gets all that stuff free."

Meg didn't like to be challenged by her little sister. "You wanna hear about the girl, right, Dorie? Then don't digress." That was a word Dorie might not know. Could she be embarrassed into silence?

Meg waited. Dorie stood there frowning and slung one hip to the side in silent response. Meg went on. "Okay. I'd just won a WETA lunch box — which is sort of boring, Dorie, but I'm talking about *financially*, it's worth more than the ten-cent ticket." Dorie still said nothing. "Anyway, I was standing in line again because I wanted to win a ghostwriter set, you know, like the one I already have except the ink's dried up? It was a nice one — a ghostwriter pen, developer pen, pad of paper — all inclusive."

"Can I talk now?" Dorie asked.

3

"Yeah."

"So she won the ghostwriter set?"

"Yeah. She was right in front of me in line. I couldn't believe it."

"What's so weird about that? Besides, she doesn't look weird, except for that hat. It's too hot for a hat." Dorie jumped and turned at the same time. It was a good hopscotch maneuver, which she followed up with three one-footed hops, then a two-footed landing, then three hops again, on down the flagstones.

Meg sighed. Lately, she'd found herself longing for the good old days when Dorie had been a placid little girl who hung on every word her big sister said. Now that Dorie was nine and Meg was eleven, things had changed. Their mother said that Dorie was trying to narrow the gap — an impossibility in Meg's view. How could Dorie eliminate even one of the 740 days that separated their births? When Meg was ninety-eight, Dorie would still be only ninety-six. It was a comforting thought. Their mother had asked Meg to be patient and include Dorie in things whenever possible, and Meg had promised to try, though she doubted it would do any good.

"I haven't got to the weird part, Dorie," Meg said as patiently as she knew how to Dorie's flying figure.

Now that she thought about it, Meg did have to agree with Dorie about the girl's looks. Her

4

features were angular but pleasant. Meg's mother would have said she had nice face bones — high cheeks, a strong chin, and wide-set blue eyes. Her skin was light, almost colorless. She wore her hair straight back from her face in a long, thick braid. It was pulled back so tight that when Meg had stood in line behind her, she wondered whether it gave the girl a headache.

Meg raised her voice so Dorie could hear. "I tried to trade her, told her the set was worth only $2.98, that you could do the same thing with lemon juice. She should've taken my lunch box. It's worth at least five dollars."

In fact, at the carnival, Meg had tried every persuasive tactic she knew. She'd even stood there on one leg, steady as a crane, open lunch box balanced on her knee, extolling the virtues of the red, white, and blue thermos.

Now Dorie was on the way back, hopping and jumping, pigtails flying, elbows bent, fists clenched.

"When I showed her the inside of the lunch box, she froze. It was the weirdest thing — like there was a tarantula or scorpion in it. Then she went off in a huge, black limousine. She never did say anything. How could a kid be so scared of a lunch box?"

Meg remembered how the girl had strode purposefully away across the playground to meet a man dressed in a business suit so dark, it might

5

have been black. They exchanged no words, but marched together up the hill away from the carnival toward the long, dark limousine. It was completely out of place among the other brightly colored parked cars, like a great black beetle in a nest of ladybugs.

Meg had stood there watching as the girl, without a backward glance, slipped into the backseat of the limousine. The man had slammed the door behind her and climbed into the driver's seat. The limousine had moved away slowly from the curb. With its darkened windows, it had reminded Meg of a hearse.

Meg shifted on her front stoop. Dorie, exhausted and hot, flopped down beside her. Dorie's face was only a shade lighter than the red ribbons tied around her pigtails. Chins in hands, elbows on knees, both girls stared hard at the house across the street.

"I've got it," Dorie said after a minute. "There were microscopic poisonous red spiders on the thermos, and she'd just landed on Earth and could see them with her alien vision?"

Meg groaned and crossed her eyes in response.

Dorie sat up straight. "Hey, remember when the Johnsons moved in? The moving men let us climb in the truck. I hope the new people across the street have nice movers. When's the van coming, do ya think?"

"There's not gonna be a van," Meg said.

"How do ya know? Could come this afternoon."

"Nope. Seven delivery trucks in three days. All new stuff. The house has got to be full," Meg said authoritatively.

"They must be rich. I wonder who they are." Dorie sounded disappointed.

"Let's see if you can figure it out. You've already picked up an important clue." Meg wished her mother could hear how patient she was being.

Dorie perked up at the praise, just as Meg knew she would.

"These are the facts," Meg continued. "One—these people *are* rich. They've bought a whole house full of that expensive Scandinavian furniture Mom likes. Two — no moving van. That means they probably had to escape quickly from wherever else they were. And they didn't want to be followed. Three — every time a new furniture shipment comes, guys inspect it with some kind of detection device, probably looking for bombs. Four — they're part of a bigger group. We know that from the inspection guys, and they also have a limousine with a driver. Now, how does that add up?"

Dorie leaned back, as far away from the house across the street as she could get without standing up, and froze in position. Only her eyes moved to Meg beside her. "Kidnappers."

"Dorie, silly, the bombs. Stick to the facts. How do bombs fit in with kidnappers?" Meg was reach-

7

ing the bottom of her deep reservoir of patience. It was one thing to humor her sister, try to develop her skills. It was another to have to put up with her totally bizarre deductions.

Meg took a deep breath. "Okay, Dorie, now listen close. I have something called a theory, and this is how is goes. The house across the street is now the headquarters of an international drug ring. Drug runners have to change headquarters fast and often. No time for moving vans. Less risk of being followed. They're very rich so they just buy new stuff."

"What about the bombs?"

"*That* is the key. All the drug people are fighting each other. So they have to be careful about bombs."

Dorie looked relieved. "Do all drug people get those special license plates?"

Meg squinted and focused carefully on the rear of the Chevy across the street. Dorie was right. The license plate was different from the ordinary blue and white D.C. plate. It had fewer and bigger numbers, and the outer edge was trimmed in red. Meg knew immediately what they were — diplomatic plates available only to foreigners working for their governments in Washington.

Just Dorie's incredible luck, to stumble by complete accident onto the most important clue of all. "That's my other theory, Dorie," Meg said quickly. "They're diplomats. They could, of course, still be drug runners with stolen plates," she finished lamely.

"I'm just glad they're not kidnappers." Dorie hadn't noticed Meg's close call.

"Well, I'm gonna keep an eye on 'em," Meg said with newfound gusto, her authority and credibility still intact.

2

The next day, Meg awoke early as usual. Breakfast was the whole Donovan family's favorite meal. It was the one time of day when everybody could be counted on to be at the same place at the same time. There was always pancakes or French toast, or eggs and sweet rolls, and a pitcher of fresh orange juice.

Meg had once said that every meal should have dessert included, just like breakfast. Meg's mother had laughed and said that she was thinking of doing just the opposite, cutting back the morning sugar intake, because she'd read that too much sugar numbs the frontal section of the brain. Meg had not raised the topic again.

Today, Meg's family was eating waffles as fast as Celia, the Donovan's housekeeper, could make them.

"It's hard for me to believe the Russians are allowing their people to live outside the compound," Mrs. Donovan was saying as Meg slid into her chair. "And to think they would put them here in our neighborhood."

"What's the compound?" Dorie asked.

"Not so much syrup, honey," Mrs. Donovan said. "It's a group of apartment and office buildings where the Russian diplomats work and live. It's not that far from here — remember the road to the soccer field? That tall wall with the barbed wire on top, on the left side of the road? That's it."

"I've always wondered what was behind that wall. It's creepy," Dorie said.

Meg's father intervened. "It was the President's idea, and the Soviets agreed. Some American families are moving into neighborhoods in Moscow, probably right this minute. It was a big deal for our governments to arrange this. It's supposed to promote better relations between our countries because we can get to know each other as neighbors."

Mr. Donovan worked on the staff of the Foreign Relations Committee of the U.S. Senate. Too often, for Meg's taste, he talked about foreign policy. But, today, she had a reason to want to hear more.

"Those are Russians across the street? Wow!" Meg smeared a large slab of butter across her first waffle. Spies. They had to be spies. That was even better than drug runners. It would require extraordinary talent to uncover professional spies.

"You know, I sort of met that girl at the carnival. But she wouldn't talk to me."

Mrs. Donovan looked affectionately at Meg. "Honey, you should go over to say hello to her."

"I dunno, Mom. She wouldn't talk to me the first time we met," Meg said, doubt in her voice. "And yesterday, when they moved in, I know she saw me sitting on the stoop but she pretended she didn't." As she spoke, it was occurring to Meg that she might well *have* to go over there if she wanted to learn more about the Russians. Get a look inside, a feel for what was really going on.

"Maybe her parents won't let her talk to Americans. Russians are Communists, you know," Dorie said to Meg.

"Thanks, Dorie," Meg said lightly. Meg could not think of a time when she didn't know that Russians are Communists. My little sister may think she's growing up, Meg thought, but I'm still light-years ahead of her when it comes to information.

Meg liked to collect information. Not just schoolbook facts, either. She liked knowing things other people had overlooked. She knew, for example, that there were forty-two stairs in her house from the third-floor study down to the basement playroom. She knew where her previously missing silver and fake-diamond-trimmed sunglasses were at this very moment — lying in a dark corner of Dorie's closet. She knew that Dorie

12

thought she didn't know. Meg liked that. It gave her a sense of power.

"Actually, only ten percent of the Russian people are card-carrying Communist party members." Mr. Donovan nodded at Dorie, taking a sip of coffee. He glanced over his cup at Meg's mother. "You know, we are living in exciting times. The Soviet Union is changing so quickly. But there's resistance in Moscow. It's hard to know what's going to happen next."

"What are Communists, anyway?" Dorie blurted out.

Meg smiled smugly as she chewed her waffle.

"Honey, you answer Dorie." Mrs. Donovan smiled at her husband. "It's one of those wheat questions." Meg's mother valued some questions more than others. The ones she did not like much, she called chaff. The difference between wheat and chaff was not always clear to Meg. Today, for example, Meg found it difficult to believe that her mother thought Dorie's ridiculous question was wheat.

"Well, communism" — Mr. Donovan cleared his throat — "it's been lots of things, really, and different in different countries. But, for starters, it's been a way of organizing an economy so that it's centrally controlled. That means the government directs everything in the economy, deciding what should be produced and what things should cost." Mr. Donovan began to lecture. "It's not

13

very efficient, and the Soviets are trying to restructure things a bit — they call it *perestroika*." Meg could tell he was warming to the topic. He twisted the Russian word in his mouth and made it sound German.

Meg tuned out as her family talked on. Dorie kept asking questions that sounded like chaff to Meg but must have been wheat because her mother and father answered them at great length. Economies and governments and politics had been topics of conversation in Meg's house ever since she could remember. She planned to have more exciting things for her children to discuss around the breakfast table.

Wistfully, Meg called up one of her favorite daydreams — it was about Sherlock Holmes. She did not consider him fiction. She felt certain the great detective had existed. She was also sure that his eccentric bachelorhood was only one of his many guises. Although she had no hard facts to support her theory, Meg just knew he had really led a happy though very private family life and had sired many children. They had sat around the breakfast table and discussed clues and cases. How could Meg be so sure of these things? Because sometimes she felt his blood in her veins.

Meg's mother interrupted her daydreams.

"Meg, you really should think about welcoming the Russian child. She must be feeling lonely and maybe a little frightened. I have a book upstairs about the Soviet Union that might be interesting," Mrs. Donovan went on. "I got it from a publisher as a promo, but haven't had a chance to read it. You can have it, if you want." Mrs. Donovan worked as the managing editor of a European travel magazine.

"Okay, Mom, thanks. If I have time." Meg stressed the "if." She found her mother's reading suggestions uneven. One of Mrs. Donovan's rules was that Meg should read one constructive book for every two adventure or mystery stories. A constructive book, according to her mother's definition, was either fiction in which the story took place sometime between the Middle Ages and 1960, or nonfiction, which reminded Meg too much of assigned reading. Meg's mother would often glance through whatever Meg was reading and would even borrow Meg's books to read herself. But, luckily, Meg read a lot of books, and Mrs. Donovan was too busy to keep an absolutely accurate tally.

After the Donovans finished breakfast, the noise level in the house rose as Meg's mother and father gathered their papers into briefcases, gave last-minute instructions to Celia, Meg, and Dorie, and headed out the door.

Just a minute later, the door slammed behind Dorie rushing off to her best friend's house, and only the soft clatter of Celia doing the breakfast dishes remained. Meg lay back on the living room couch. She had the whole day ahead of her; no school, no homework, no piano lessons, not even gym practice. She would make her bed and put away her microscope later. Her insect-parts slides were lying all over her desk upstairs and needed dusting and refiling, but there was no rush. By noon, Celia would have stacks of laundry for Meg to fold and put away in drawers. Until then, Meg would fill the morning only with things she wanted to do.

She thought about writing a letter to her best friend, Kathy, who was spending the summer in California. It would be fun writing in the code they had developed just for themselves. Kathy was a great best friend, and Meg missed her desperately now that she'd been gone for a whole week. Kathy was not scared to pass secret notes in class and, since all the kids at school liked Kathy, she always had some interesting news to share. Meg's mother might have called it gossip, but Meg considered it information. She figured Sherlock Holmes would have felt the same way.

But Meg's ghostwriter was out of ink and, besides, she didn't have any real news yet. She didn't want to tell Kathy about the spies across the street until there was progress to report.

Meg thought of calling David, but rejected the idea. She'd known him since they were babies because their parents were friends. Although he was going to spend the month of August on a ranch out West, he was home now and for all of July. But he had been over just two days before and she didn't want to be seen hanging around with him all the time. It would create the wrong impression. She didn't stop to think what the right impression might be.

Meg braced herself. She had given herself an assignment and she should not postpone it any longer. Those Russians might be up to no good already. She would visit and find out what she could. Besides, there was nothing else to do.

3

Meg stared at the peephole in the middle of the front door of the house across the street, waiting for someone to answer the bell. She carried three dark pink roses from her mother's garden, the stems wrapped in a damp paper towel and wax paper. A sharp thorn poked through, pricking the palm of her hand.

She waited for what seemed like hours. Just as she gave up and turned to go back home, the front door opened and the short, square woman Meg had seen the day before stuck her head through the opening.

"Why are you here?" The woman spoke with a heavy accent, peering at the roses as though she'd never seen anything like them before. Her round, soft face and brilliant blue eyes would have looked downright grandmotherly if, somehow, her barking voice could have been ignored.

Meg swallowed and cleared her throat. "I live

across the street, and these are roses from our garden."

The woman reached out and took the roses, holding them between her thumb and index finger. She was about to close the door but was interrupted. Her head disappeared for a moment as she shouted something in what must have been Russian to someone inside the house. The door opened wide, and the woman, motioning Meg to come in quickly, glanced behind Meg and looked up and down the street before slamming the door behind her.

She led Meg into the living room. "Please sit here." The woman motioned abruptly to a white couch that Meg had watched being delivered. It had been turned upended on the lawn while a man moved what looked like a pocket-sized calculator slowly in and out of the spaces between the springs. Meg knew it must be free of bombs, but the thought did not help her relax.

The house was dark despite the light Scandinavian furniture. Heavy brocade draperies covered the windows. If they are going to keep the drapes closed, Meg thought, they ought to buy more lamps.

She waited, sitting stiffly on the couch. She wished she still had her roses, even with the thorns. Her hands might feel more like her own if they were holding something, instead of keeping them folded in her lap like a figure in an old-fashioned portrait.

Drawers slammed upstairs, a squeaky medicine cabinet door opened and closed, a toilet flushed, and finally Meg heard someone coming down the stairs.

"My name is Irina Petrovna Lysikov." The girl entered the room with her hand outstretched toward Meg. Her tight smile and her stiff, formal bearing brought Meg to her feet, mentally groaning.

"I'm Meg Donovan. I live across the street."

Meg shook Irina's cold, dry hand. Do all Russian kids shake hands, she wondered, or just this one?

Irina took one of the two chairs facing the couch and rested both hands on the arms of the chair. "It is a pleasure to meet you. This is the first time I have met an American teenager. You are a teenager, aren't you?"

Perhaps Irina had forgotten they'd met before, Meg thought. Maybe she's nearsighted. Anyway, today she didn't resemble the girl at the carnival who had stared in fright at a lunch box. She seemed to be taking charge.

"No. Well, almost," Meg replied. "I brought your mother some roses from the garden. They are my mother's favorite."

"Oh. Mrs. Bugayev. She is not my mother. She is our housekeeper," Irina replied. "My mother is dead."

"That's too bad," Meg mumbled. This is not going well, she thought. First, she sits there like a grand inquisitor and next, I bring up her dead mother. Meg was grateful that Mrs. Bugayev had walked into the room and placed a tray with a teapot, cups and saucers, and a plate of sugar cookies on the coffee table. Meg leaned forward and concentrated on putting milk and sugar into her tea without spilling it.

Mrs. Bugayev did not join them. Instead, she sat in an adjoining room and knitted. Meg could not see her but she could hear the needles clicking from time to time. Didn't some lady during the French Revolution knit the names of traitors into her sweater? And later weren't they executed? Now, don't get spooked, Meg told herself. It's just an ordinary house with a few Russians in it.

The silence began to bother Meg. "Where are you going to school next year?" she asked.

"To the embassy school. Where do you go to school? Do you go to school with any poor people?"

"I just graduated from sixth grade. I'll be going to the junior high down the street next year," Meg replied guardedly.

She did not answer the question about poor people because she did not know what to say. But she had a feeling that the question was not just a friendly inquiry. The follow-up attack came immediately.

"There are so many rich people here exploiting

21

the labor of poor people," Irina stated. She made no gestures with her hands as she talked, but kept them pressed on the arms of the chair. "I remember reading in my newspaper at home that the richest one to two percent of Americans receive twenty-four percent of all household income. Black people and Spanish-speaking people are the poorest, and Americans take advantage of them."

"Black people *are* Americans. And so are lots of Hispanics," Meg pointed out. But she didn't want to be rude, so she added quickly, "Well, there is some poverty, but we're trying to get rid of it." She felt confused, caught between her guest manners and her desire to hold her ground in this bizarre conversation. Could guest manners be forgotten when the hostess is rude? Meg intended to ask her mother at the next opportunity. That might be a wheat question.

"We do not have rich people making money from the labor of the poor in the Soviet Union," Irina said. She grew straighter and stiffer in her chair as she talked. "Everyone is equal."

Irina's statement reminded Meg of the drama class play. Meg and Kathy had been in the audience and had not been able to control their laughter at how different from normal the kids sounded when they spoke their lines. Formal, and stiff, and memorized. That was the way Irina sounded to Meg right now, but Meg didn't feel like laughing.

"Our Declaration of Independence says we are all created equal, too. Everybody has an equal opportunity to get rich, but not everybody does." Now that's a decent point, Meg congratulated herself.

Irina ignored it. "In the Soviet Union, the people control everything. We own the factories and the farms and the stores. Nobody can take advantage of anybody else."

Meg grasped for ideas. "Basketball players are rich, and a lot of them are from poor families. And there's the lottery, too. Anybody can win that."

"Twenty percent of the people in the United States live at poverty or near-poverty levels," Irina said triumphantly. "That is a statistic from *your* newspaper."

Meg wanted to change the subject. She felt stung by Irina's arguments, as though there might be a good chance that she, Meg, was personally responsible for all the poverty in the United States. "How come you speak English so well?"

"My mother was a teacher of English and a great patriot. I think she loved our country more than anything. Except me, of course. She died two years ago of cancer." She hesitated. "I was her best student," she added more quietly.

"Oh," Meg said. She couldn't think of anything else to say or ask. She wondered how soon she could escape this house. Her mission was a failure. She'd uncovered nothing. Irina certainly wasn't a spy. She was too direct, too offensive. She had no subtlety.

Irina's face brightened. "Papa's taking me shopping to buy some American clothes. Where should we go?" Irina pulled a piece of paper and pen from the pocket of her dress.

"Oh. Shopping. There's a great mall called Mazza Gallerie down Western Avenue about a mile." Meg's mind wandered. Better watch out, Irina, Mazza Gallerie's full of rich people.

"How do you spell that?" Irina concentrated on her writing.

Meg was in the middle of spelling "Mazza" when their conversation was interrupted by the sound of a key turning in the front door.

"Papa!" Irina shouted and shoved the slip of paper into her pocket. She ran to the door with her arms outstretched and was quickly enveloped in a bear hug, her feet off the floor. Her father laughed heartily at her enthusiasm as he looked over her shoulder at Meg on the couch.

He said something in Russian and then spoke in English. "And who is this young lady?"

"This is Meg Donovan from across the street, the first neighbor to visit us." Irina turned back toward Meg, smoothing her dress. "Meg, this is my father."

Meg reached out her hand and felt it disappear in Mr. Lysikov's. Everything about the man seemed large. His dark hair was unparted,

24

combed straight back from his forehead. It was so thick it gave him an extra inch or two above what must have been his six-foot height. His eyebrows were black and hairs curled every which way. He was obviously making an effort to speak softly, controlling a voice that would otherwise boom through the house.

"Irina has so much to learn about the United States," he said, looking directly into Meg's eyes. "You look as though you would be an excellent teacher."

Meg shifted her weight. Fat chance, she thought. I think we're natural enemies. But she said, "I, uh, might be able to try." She was glad when he finally let go of her hand. "I have to be getting home now. I have to set the table for lunch."

Irina stepped forward and put her arms around Meg, hugging her tight and putting her face first on one of Meg's cheeks and then on the other. Since there was nothing else to do with them, Meg placed her hands stiffly on Irina's shoulders. She backed away as quickly as she could. Still bruised from their discussion, Meg found Irina's gesture hollow and disagreeable. She heard herself promising to return and was proud to have enough presence of mind not to say soon.

As Meg hurried across the street to her own house, she looked back and saw Irina and her father standing in their doorway, waving. Mr.

Lysikov was handsome and friendly, not at all how she expected a Russian spy would be. He acted as though he adored his daughter and wanted her to make friends.

But, she reminded herself, after all, he was a professional. His job was deception. He was, now that Meg really thought about it, *too* friendly. But of course only a clever observer, someone with a mind like Sherlock Holmes, for example, would notice that he was too friendly. Yes, she decided, Mr. Lysikov was definitely a spy. She would never be deceived by his charm. And she made herself another promise. She would be ready next time Irina went on the attack.

4

Through lunch, Meg did not feel like talking. Luckily she didn't have to. Dorie brought her animal joke book to the table and asked Celia riddles. The book was already dog-eared when Meg passed it along to her sister a couple of years ago. Meg knew that Celia, who'd been with the Donovan family since Meg's birth, had heard those riddles at least a hundred times. But Celia pretended not to know the answers and laughed as hard as Dorie when Dorie delivered the well-worn punch lines.

Meg went over her conversation with Irina as she worked her way through tuna fish, cottage cheese, and an English muffin. By the time she was finished, she was angry. After all, she'd taken the trouble to go over there. She'd even brought roses. What did Irina do? She had blasted Meg with insults about the United States.

Meg knew she'd have to see Irina again. Only

through Irina could she gather sufficient information to reveal the spy in their midst. And Meg was not the sort of person to shirk an assignment just because it entailed a few hardships.

But that didn't mean she and that girl had to be friends, or even that Meg had to sit meekly turning the other cheek. Meg wanted her own ammunition. She needed to know more about the Soviet Union. Surely it wasn't perfect. If she found stuff that was good enough, she might even make a few large placards and pound their posts into her front yard at just the right angle so Irina could read them from across the street.

She found her mother's book about the Soviet Union and settled into the overstuffed chair near the front window. She intended to read and keep an eye on Irina's house at the same time.

Meg skipped through the first chapters on early Russian history and began with the chapter on the Communist party. She read that party members had special privileges. They had the best housing, best jobs, and even shopped in special stores stocked with the best products. So much for equality in the Soviet Union, Meg thought. She planned her first placard.

WE PAID FOR THAT EXPENSIVE
SCANDINAVIAN FURNITURE.
— The People

Meg read on. Shoddy consumer goods, cold weather, and official disapproval of T-shirts on teenagers made life in the Soviet Union seem to Meg to be dreary indeed. Young people who dyed their hair orange or purple or blue or wore unusual clothes were called "hooligans" and were harassed by the police or even thrown in jail.

If she lived in Russia, would she actually be criticized on the street or harassed by police for wearing her favorite T-shirt, the one she had bought with twenty weeks of allowance money, the one with sequins sewn on by hand? Another placard formed in Meg's mind.

PRESERVE HOOLIGANISM —
Wear a Sequined T-shirt

Meg began skimming. She needed a zinger, something to wrap up her arguments in one sentence. Eventually, she read that people who criticize the government or Soviet way of life are considered mental deviants and are put in psychiatric hospitals. That would put Bruce Springsteen in a straitjacket. Meg wondered if Irina could see the message if she wrote it in glitter glue.

FREE THE SANE

Meg felt she was finally ready for another discussion with Irina. "Your country is the social equivalent of bad breath," Meg imagined herself saying to a shocked Irina. "It is *boring*." Irina would fall to her knees, the weight of the truth bringing her down to defeat.

Meg slammed the book shut. If there was going to be another superpower skirmish, she was now prepared to fight.

Later that day, after Mrs. Donovan came home from work, Meg took her usual perch on the toilet lid to talk as her mother showered. "That Russian girl's a real pain. She really hates the United States and she thinks the Soviet Union's perfect," Meg reported loudly so her mother could hear.

"Doesn't surprise me," Mrs. Donovan shouted back. "The Soviets aren't exactly fans of ours, though we're trying now to improve relations. But I'm glad you went over there, honey," Mrs. Donovan spoke more softly, peeking around the shower curtain. "Were you nervous, meeting a Russian?"

"Nah. But I don't want to sit through any of her lectures for a long time," Meg said. "Mom, what should we do about all the poor people in this country?"

"Honey, that's a wheat question. Can you wait till I'm finished?" Mrs. Donovan disappeared again into the shower.

"Irina — that's her name — says there aren't any poor people in the Soviet Union," Meg shouted. The noise of the shower drowned out

Meg's next sentence. "We had a kind of debate and I think she won."

"I'm no expert on the Soviet Union, but I don't think that's true," Meg's mother shouted back. "Their standard of living is much lower in general, and right now they have terrible economic problems." Mrs. Donovan paused. "Our system is more productive overall. We just need to figure out how to distribute the wealth more fairly while still providing incentives to create new wealth." Mrs. Donovan turned off the shower. "Did you get all that?"

"Sure, Mom," Meg said as her mother emerged from the shower. Meg gave her the towel she'd been holding in her lap. Would Irina think it was weird if Meg brought her mother over for the next debate?

"If nothing else, Irina has you thinking about something important. Here you are, living in Washington, D.C., where public policy is made, and you've always hated talking about issues. Maybe Irina will make you want to be a senator, cutie, and the FBI will have to find someone else to lead it into the twenty-first century." Her mother leaned over and pecked Meg on the forehead.

"No chance, Mom." Meg knew her career plans amused her mother and father. She put up with it gracefully. She figured that all great people had had to put up with some ridicule, especially when they were young, and had only plans, no accomplishments.

Meg's mother laughed and switched on her blow-dryer, making further conversation impossible.

Still sitting on the toilet lid, Meg stuck her hands in her pockets, leaned back, and stretched out her legs, intending to wait until her mother finished. She pulled a piece of notepaper from her pocket, saw that it was blank, and started to toss it into the wastebasket.

Then she stopped. The piece of paper looked just the size and shape of the pad that came with the ghostwriter set. But she hadn't used her set for weeks, ever since her ghostwriter had run out of ink. Besides, how could a piece of paper from the ghostwriter pad get into the pocket of a pair of pants that had just been washed the previous day? Then Meg remembered. Irina had the same disappearing ink set. She'd won it at the carnival.

Meg jumped up and ran to her bedroom. She found her developer pen in her desk drawer.

Sorry. We were being watched. I hope we shall be friends, the note read. It was signed *Irina*.

A secret message. Meg smiled a big, wide smile. It was really too good to be true. The Sherlock Holmes portion of her blood tingled. Her fingers itched for her own ghostwriter pen. Then she remembered — it was all used up.

She fell on her bottom bunk bed from where

she could see Irina's house through the window. Excitement scrambled her thoughts. She had to get another ghostwriter — and quick. How had Irina done it? She had written the message and got it into Meg's pocket undetected. Meg remembered that awkward embrace. That was it. She must have slipped it in then. What did Irina mean? Who was watching?

Maybe Irina was not going to be such a pain after all. Meg was too single-minded to be put off her self-assigned mission — uncovering that Soviet spy. But maybe she could have some real fun with Irina at the same time. She had no aversion whatsoever to mixing business and pleasure.

5

The next morning when Meg returned home from the toy store with a new ghostwriter, she found a message from David. He wanted her to go down to the Mall to the Museum of Natural History with him. Meg telephoned her mother and, after the usual admonitions — no bicycles downtown, take the subway, stay together, keep at least twenty-five cents for an emergency phone call — permission was granted.

Within an hour, David had arrived by bicycle and stood, skateboard in hand, on Meg's front stoop. He was wearing a yellow T-shirt with HOT BUTTER written in red script across his chest.

"You're riding your skateboard to the subway stop?" Meg asked.

"Yeah. Is that okay?"

"Sure." Actually, it was fine with Meg because David on a skateboard was the same height as she. It made conversation difficult, but eliminated

Meg's embarrassment at towering above David for the mile-long walk through the neighborhood to the subway station.

On the way, David rode first on the street, and then up onto the sidewalk, and back onto the street. At one point, he started on the sidewalk a block ahead of Meg, gathered speed, then stopped directly in front of her, flipping his skateboard into his hands and taking an exaggerated bow.

"Not bad, David. You've learned some new tricks," Meg said. With only a wide grin in response, he was off again, whistling "Yankee Doodle," his shoelaces flapping behind him.

Meg's parents liked to say that Meg and David had known each other since before they were born. The two sets of parents had met in childbirth classes and had been friends ever since. Meg's baby book was peppered with pictures of David— David kissing Meg's bald infant head, David and Meg in the baby pool, David and Meg building a sand castle at the beach.

David lived in the next neighborhood over. He went to a different school and, though they were only two weeks apart in age, David had always been a grade behind Meg because his birthday fell beyond the deadline for starting kindergarten.

Meg had always liked David. He was not at all like her best friend Kathy, with whom she shared her most secret thoughts. She and David never sat around and talked. They rode bikes, ice-skated, practiced soccer.

Lately, being with David reminded her of those carefree days when she'd had nothing more on her mind than the next ice-cream cone. She'd begun to think of herself as more sophisticated than David, mainly because her interests had branched beyond food. But she was not about to give up their good times together. Meg figured her times with David were sort of like a second childhood.

"What does your mom think about your new haircut?" Meg asked when they were finally in the subway and could talk. David wore his hair in a moderate punk crew cut, with a long-haired section down the middle of the back of his head, and a swatch of hair in the front about two inches long that he kept greased and combed back.

David laughed. "She made me pay for it myself. She didn't say anything about it when I got home, though, so I guess she likes it okay."

"Bet you my mom will say something."

"Yeah, she might. But she might not." David slouched back in his seat, his eyes glued to the subway ceiling. Meg knew he was calculating the odds.

"It's probably a quarter bet. Want it?" he asked.

"If she says something about it, *anything* about it, you owe me a quarter, right?" Meg had lost to David more than once on a technicality, and she wanted to make sure the terms of the bet were clear.

"Yup. I'm betting on your mom's good manners. You're betting she won't be able to keep her mouth shut when she sees it." David crossed his arms and looked smug.

Put that way, Meg figured she was probably on the wrong side of the bet. Her mother's rule was that if you can't say something nice, don't say it at all. It was hard to imagine her mother saying something nice about David's haircut. Oh, well, Meg thought, what was a quarter now that she'd just gotten a raise in her allowance. She had over three dollars in her purse at this very moment to spend on a snack or something interesting in the museum shop. She accepted the bet.

They switched trains at Metro Center and clambered out at the Smithsonian stop. As they got off the escalator, Meg paused to take in the view of the Mall from the solid, stately Capitol to the slender needle of the Washington Monument, connected by a long stretch of green grass bordered by the old red castle and the great gray buildings that made up the Smithsonian. Tourists were everywhere. They licked ice-cream cones and pushed baby strollers or carried kids on their shoulders. Meg liked tourists — Californians, Texans, Iowans. They traveled thousands of miles to see her hometown, a city that belonged just as much to them as to her. The only major difference, really, was that they traveled hours, sometimes days, and all Meg had to do was take a fifteen-minute subway ride.

"Which museum?" asked David. "American History? Science and Industry? Art — modern, traditional, African, Asian? Sculpture? Air and Space?"

They went through this ritual every time, even though both of them knew they would go straight to the Museum of Natural History to see the dinosaurs. Today, David was especially expansive. He stood there gesturing toward each museum as he talked. Meg caught the mood. It was a whole world waiting to be explored.

"After the triceratops, the universe," she said grandly. David grinned back and they wove their way through the tourists to the Museum of Natural History.

Once inside, they went directly to the dinosaur exhibit. They considered themselves experts. They could tell the museum-made bones from the real thing and were able to spot small changes in the exhibits immediately. They were following closely the ongoing debate about dinosaurs and sided wholeheartedly with the scientists who argued that dinosaurs were warm-blooded, fairly intelligent creatures related more closely to birds than to lizards. They had decided when they were seven that dinosaurs were fairly intelligent. How could dumb, cold-blooded creatures inspire such love from so many children? It was gratifying to find that the scientific community was finally catching up.

"Hey, there's the Human Library," a voice called after them as they left the exhibit. The words "Human Library" echoed softly from the marble walls and floors and moved upward to the lofty ceiling where they mixed with the coughing, sneezing, foot shuffling, and chattering of the other museum-goers.

Meg recognized Lacey Darcy's voice before she turned around. Lacey Darcy had been the most popular girl in Meg's first-grade class and nothing had changed since. Meg turned around to see Lacey strolling toward her, hand in hand with Kenny Davis. Kenny towered at least a foot above Lacey. Meg and Kathy had watched *Gone With the Wind* eleven times on video, and they both agreed that Kenny Davis was Rhett Butler reincarnated without a mustache.

"Uh-oh. It's Beauty and the Beast," Meg said so both Lacey and Kenny could hear. "How come you're not at camp, beast?" Meg addressed Lacey. At least she'd thought of a comeback.

Lacey laughed easily. She threw her head back and her blonde hair rearranged itself over her shoulders, falling into graceful curls at the ends.

Her face is not that pretty, Meg thought for about the hundredth time in her life. She had made a study of that face over the years. Lacey's eyes were too close together, and her pug nose had been cute when she was little but now looked silly to Meg. Too bad none of the boys seemed to notice.

"Next week. I didn't know you had a little brother. Hi," Lacey said to David.

"I'm not her brother." David grinned broadly at Lacey and stuck his hands in his pockets. A second later, he pulled his shoulders back, pulled out his right hand, and offered it to Kenny. Kenny laughed in surprise and shook hands with David. He even bowed a little, as though he were humoring a little kid.

"Oh, sorry." Lacey looked genuinely embarrassed. "Well, gotta go. Don't get ahead of us all this summer, Meg. Not too many books." She waved her free hand, turned to go, and then giggled at something Kenny had said so quietly Meg could not hear.

"How come they call you the Human Library?" David asked, looking down at his feet and kicking an invisible pebble. Meg knew he had felt awkward with Lacey and Kenny. She had not felt that smooth herself.

"Oh, it's just a joke. Everybody sort of got a nickname in the yearbook and that was mine." She'd been looking forward to having what she thought was a really good picture of herself in the sixth-grade yearbook — a soft smile with no gums showing like they used to in pictures of her when she was a kid. Her blue eyes were crinkling in the corners just like her mother's. She thought she looked at least fifteen in that picture. She'd been shocked when she'd seen the name the yearbook editors had put in dark black type just below her smiling face.

"It's just a joke," Meg repeated. "It doesn't bother me."

"It's supposed to mean you're smart or something?" David said. "You don't seem that smart to me." David had cheered up quickly, too quickly for Meg.

"Thanks a lot, David." Meg glared at him. Lacey and Kenny are probably wondering whether he's my boyfriend and they're laughing about how short he is right this very second, Meg thought.

"Just trying to make you feel better about it. Hey, how about a hot fudge sundae in the East Building café?"

"Sure. Why not?" Meg replied grumpily. The East Building was part of the Smithsonian's National Gallery of Art, but was a separate, modern structure, full of angles and glass, and connected to the main building by an underground walkway. Meg liked the café there and, even though she'd outgrown David's obsession with food, a hot fudge sundae did sound comforting.

It was a long walk and skateboard ride along the Mall. The sidewalk slammed the heat back at pedestrians, and the humidity wrapped them in a wet gauze. Noonday joggers moved grimly past Meg and David.

Meg felt instant relief when she entered the East Building. It was cool and open. The huge red mobile, designed by Alexander Calder, turned slowly in its off-center position in the soaring central court. The mobile seemed to capture the heat and the haze outside and transform it into a dreamy, lazy summer day inside. The encounter with Lacey and Kenny, though it still stung, seemed removed from this calm, cool atmosphere.

As Meg and David walked along the upper-level bridge to the café entrance, they paused for a moment to look down.

Like an oil painting in motion, Meg thought. People in their bright summer clothes walked up and down the two flights of stairs and along the polished marble-granite floor under the mobile. People stopped to admire exhibits on the walls. People entered the central court from the low-ceiling anteroom, pointing, talking, always in motion. Meg wondered whether the architect had seen this in his mind before the building was ever built.

Two men in business suits caught Meg's eye. One was leaning against the wall over by an enormous, bright tapestry, and the other was facing him. They were talking intently. To Meg, they seemed oblivious to the enchantment of their surroundings.

Meg started. One was Mr. Lysikov, Irina's father, and he was listening, head cocked to one side, to the animated speech of the other man.

"David, I know this is weird. But would you please go down quick by that tapestry and see if you can hear what those men are saying?" Meg nodded her head in the direction of the two men as David looked at her quizzically.

David shrugged. "Sure." He went loping down the steps, galloped out of sight under the bridge, and reappeared in front of the tapestry on the other side. He stopped abruptly in front of the information card next to the hanging and near the two men. Almost immediately, Mr. Lysikov handed the other man a package and shook his hand. They exchanged a few more words and quickly separated, one walking toward the front entrance, and the other going down the stairs toward the underground passage to the main building.

"The tall guy thanked the short guy for his help, and the short guy said he would be in touch as soon as any information became available," David reported to Meg between gasps for breath when he returned. "That's all I could hear. They left right after I got there. What's going on?"

"I know. I saw." Meg was disappointed that the men chose to leave so soon. Had David been so obvious they'd suspected him of eavesdropping? She and David entered the Terrace Café and chose

43

a small table near the window so they could look out over the mall. "The tall man is a new neighbor of ours. He's from the Soviet Union."

"You think he's a spy?" David asked after he listened to Meg's story with wide eyes. Meg left out only the secret note from Irina.

"Yup. And I think we've caught him red-handed."

"Wow! We could get a Medal of Honor from the President! What do you think we should say at our press conference? You could tell the part about living across from them. I'll tell how I sneaked up on them and overheard their secret conversation. Do you think it was in code? Maybe not; it seemed normal. Do you think they knew I was listening?"

David was already hogging the glory.

"Hey, David. You can't tell anybody about this."

"Why not? We have to. It's for our country. I'm sure that guy's a spy."

"We'll tell the right people at the right time. But we have to figure out how to do it. If we do it the wrong way, we could mess up everything." Meg was fast-pedaling.

"Mess up what?"

Then it came to her. "Maybe our government can talk him into being a counterspy, and we can give him wrong information. He'll pass it on, and his government will believe it. It happens all the time, you know." She tried to sound matter-of-fact.

"I dunno." David did not sound convinced.

"He's my spy. I found him first." She felt a little sheepish using that old argument, but she was desperate to retain her leading role as spycatcher. To her surprise, it worked.

"Aw, well, okay." David resigned himself to their long-standing rule from childhood — finders keepers.

They paid for their hot fudge sundaes and headed home. On the subway, David described the pictures he had seen of the ranch where he was going to spend the month of August. Ordinarily, Meg would have wanted to know all the smallest details. But now she sat slumped in her seat, her arms folded, staring out the black window of the subway train. Now that she'd caught a spy, she had to figure out what to do with him.

When they got back to Meg's house, she was irritated to see David's bike in front of her house. She had not paid much attention to where he had left it earlier in the day, but now it seemed to fill the whole front yard.

"David, I wish you'd park your bike around back. I told you that before, remember? I don't want all my friends from school to see it." In her glum mood, she imagined Lacey Darcy and Kenny

45

Davis walking by the front of the house, pointing at the bike, and falling onto the grass in uncontrolled laughter.

David grimaced. "That is really dumb."

"It is not dumb. You would understand it if you went to my school."

"You mean I would understand it if I'd just graduated from sixth grade instead of fifth?" David's voice cracked.

"David, don't get mad." Meg knew she'd offended David, but her impatience was greater than her sympathy.

David stuck his hands in his pockets, his skateboard still under one arm. "You're the only girl I know who isn't weird. And now you're getting weird, too." He turned quickly and threw his skateboard into his bicycle basket with a crash. He swung himself onto the seat and rode down the short embankment to the sidewalk.

Am I getting weird? Meg asked herself. One thing was for sure. David had never before acted so angry with her.

6

"You look like you've lost your best friend." Meg's father looked up from his computer monitor and pushed himself back from his desk. Stacks of papers and books surrounded him in his third-floor study.

Meg slumped down in her father's brown leather reading chair. "I may as well have. Kathy's in California, and David and I had a fight."

"Oh? A lovers' quarrel?"

Meg frowned and leaned forward to stand up and leave.

"Sorry, honey. Didn't mean to tease," Mr. Donovan said more quietly.

Meg accepted her father's apology and fell back in the chair.

"So what's the matter?"

"Did you ever have a friend who was a girl but she didn't want to be your girlfriend?"

"Let's see." Meg's father thought for a moment. "No, at your age, I didn't have girlfriends or friends who were girls. I had my sister and her friends, of course, but they seemed like little kids."

"Later I had just girlfriends, I think," he continued. "Until I met your mother. It seems she's always been both a friend and a girlfriend. Bet this is about David, isn't it?"

"Yeah. I don't want people to think he's my boyfriend. I want a real boyfriend, and if everybody sees me hanging around with David, I'll never get one."

"Honey, I don't think *everybody* is paying that close attention to the kids you hang around with."

"All the other girls already have boyfriends. I haven't even been on a date." The more she talked about it, the more bleak her situation seemed to Meg.

"*All* the girls? That seems unlikely. Besides, don't I remember you going to the movies and duckpin bowling last spring with a group of kids that included boys? And those parties you went to — the dancing parties?"

"Yeah. But nobody really likes me. We think Kirk might like Kathy. We don't think any of the boys like me."

"You mean 'like' as a girlfriend?"

"Yeah."

"Well, it's hard for me to believe that's true, Meg. Maybe it is. Maybe they need a few years to develop some taste. Take it from me, my dear

48

girl, you're going to make some lucky man one humdinger of a partner someday."

"Oh, Dad, I hope the boys in junior high are more mature." Meg sighed.

Mr. Donovan started to say something and stopped. He smiled and started again. "Well. Maybe David could disguise himself as a postman. The problem would be the skateboard — how to camouflage the skateboard." Mr. Donovan leaned back in his desk chair, thinking.

"That's not funny, Dad."

"I don't have any other brilliant ideas. I suppose you could just stop seeing David."

Not see David. No phone calls. No bike rides together to the library or down to the creek or to the ice-cream parlor. No more trips to the Smithsonian museums. All of July without David.

"I guess I'll just have to tell him why I don't want his bike out front."

"Mmmm. Good idea." Mr. Donovan turned back to his keyboard. "Tell him to be discreet. We don't want the neighbors to think nothing is going on between the two of you."

Her father's sense of humor was decidedly bizarre. Meg decided to ignore what he'd said. A reaction would only encourage him. "Dad, you know one other thing? I think the Russian man across the street is a spy, but I don't know how to turn him in. Should I just call the FBI, d'ya think?"

Mr. Donovan stopped typing but did not take his eyes off the monitor. "He probably is a spy. Many of the people at the Soviet embassy are. They're either members of the KGB secret police, or KGB informers."

Meg knew a brush-off when she heard one. "Yeah, but I saw him giving a package, the payoff probably, to somebody." Meg began to tell her father how she'd seen Mr. Lysikov at the East Building that morning.

Meg's father sighed quietly and turned his chair from his desk to face Meg again and listen.

"The other man said that he would be in touch as soon as information became available?" Mr. Donovan asked. "That doesn't necessarily mean the information's secret. Maybe he was just offering to let Mr. Lysikov know when something useful to the Soviets appears again in the *Congressional Record*."

Meg had heard that tone before. She'd heard her father complain just the other day to her mother, "The Soviets can read American newspaper stories on the health of the President's nose. They can view his stomach from the inside out on TV. But when a Soviet leader doesn't appear in public for a month, we don't know whether he's on vacation or dead."

Meg frowned. "So you don't think Mr. Lysikov was stealing secrets?"

"Seems unlikely. Not that it never happens.

Maybe it was just a member of his staff reporting to him."

"In the East Building?" Meg tried one more time.

"That does seem a little odd. But you can't go running to the FBI with so little information. They wouldn't be able to do much more than they're probably already doing to watch the guy." Mr. Donovan changed the subject. "Meg, the Chairman is not going to have much to say to the Secretary of State at the hearing next week if I don't get this work finished."

Meg folded her arms with a shrug. It was disappointing that her father took her evidence so lightly.

"Say, why don't you check with your mom to see if your Russian friend can come for dinner sometime?" Meg's father asked. "I'd like to meet her, too."

Meg brightened. Her father had just provided the excuse she needed to get back in touch with Irina. "Okay, Dad. Thanks. You can go back to work now." She kissed him on the cheek as she left. If her father wanted more evidence, she'd get it. She would call Irina first thing the next morning.

Later that evening, Meg called David.

"I'm sorry I got mad at you this afternoon, David. I don't want you to park your bike out front all the time because I don't want anybody to get the wrong idea — that we're boyfriend and girlfriend, you know." Meg held her breath, waiting for David to get mad at her again.

"How could anybody think that? You're too tall," David responded. "Besides, I already have a girlfriend."

"You do?" Meg was surprised. David had never told her about a girlfriend. Not that they sat around and shared secrets, but Meg thought she knew the fundamental things going on in David's life, and having a girlfriend was pretty fundamental.

"Yeah. I had to. It was self-defense. Girls from my class kept calling me, so I figured I'd choose one and then the rest would leave me alone." David laughed. He sounded embarrassed.

"Who'd you choose?"

"A girl who's away for the whole summer." Now David was bragging. "The phone calls have stopped, and I have a girlfriend I never have to do anything about."

"I suppose she's short." Meg knew what it was like to be taller than David. But until now she hadn't thought of it from David's point of view.

"Uh-huh. Shortest in the class."

David is so popular among the girls at his school, he has to take self-defense measures, Meg thought to herself as she hung up. She went to bed that night wondering why her life seemed so much more complicated than his.

7

On the phone the next morning, the Soviet embassy would not give Meg the Lysikovs' number. This was as she expected. Why would they give away information about one of their top spies? Just to prove her point, she kept politely insisting and was transferred to four different offices before she finally reached someone who sounded like Mr. Lysikov's secretary. The secretary said the number was not available. It made Meg grin into the receiver as she said thank-you and hung up.

Now what to do? She really did need to get in touch with Irina. She leaned back against one of the kitchen stools, folded her arms, and stared at the phone.

"Why don't you try directory assistance?" Dorie spoke without looking up from the paint-by-number picture she was working on at the kitchen table. Bright-colored blotches formed the vague outline of a bird on the canvas in front of her.

"Can't hurt." Meg quickly dialed 411, gave the spelling of Lysikov and the street, and was told to hold the line. In an instant, a computer gave her the number in a halting, mechanical voice. Meg scrambled for the pencil on the telephone counter and quickly jotted down the number.

"Dorie, you're brilliant!" Meg beamed at her little sister, who shrugged and smiled almost shyly back. What a quirky development. Meg hadn't expected Mr. Lysikov's number to be listed with directory assistance. It must be significant. She put it in the back of her mind to analyze later and dialed the number.

"Hello. May I speak to Irina?" Meg had hoped Irina would answer, but found herself talking to Mrs. Bugayev instead.

"Who is this?" Mrs. Bugayev asked gruffly.

"It's Meg Donovan. I came to your house for tea the other day." Meg wondered whether "your house" was the proper thing to say.

"No. Irina is not allowed to talk on the telephone. Good-bye." Mrs. Bugayev hung up.

"That woman is dreadful," Meg said under her breath. She wandered into the dining room and looked out the window at the house across the street. Now how could she get in touch with Irina?

She was not going to knock on the front door again without being invited. She had her new ghostwriter set in her pocket. Maybe she could send Irina a disappearing-ink note. But if Mrs. Bugayev saw her drop it off, she might pick it up and figure out the secret. *That* Meg wanted to avoid at all costs.

The phone rang. Meg hurried to the kitchen to answer. With no response to Meg's "hello," Mrs. Bugayev's voice boomed through the receiver. "You are coming to tea this morning at eleven?"

"Uh. Yes, I can. Thank you," Meg answered.

"Good-bye." Mrs. Bugayev hung up.

Later that morning, after putting on a fresh white T-shirt and transferring her ghostwriter to the pocket of her clean pair of cutoff jeans, Meg was ushered into the house with a stiff nod of greeting from Mrs. Bugayev.

"Irina is in the garden," Mrs. Bugayev said, leading Meg down the short hall beside the staircase. Meg took the opportunity to look for clues, hidden cameras, and microphones. Irina had said they were being watched. How, Meg wondered, and by whom? Meg glanced in the kitchen. Not much to see except a sink piled with dirty dishes and trash overflowing the bin. Maybe Mrs. Bugayev knits well, Meg thought, following the broad, short form of the housekeeper through the screened porch to the patio.

"Hello. I'm glad you came," Irina said. She stood as Meg came toward her. She was wearing a soft pink cotton dress with a white collar.

Meg wished she'd worn a dress. After seeing Irina, her shorts and T-shirt made her limbs feel long and skinny.

"I hope it's not too hot for you on the patio. We can have some privacy here," Irina added and sat back down.

"Oh, no, it's fine," Meg said. "I got your note."

"Oh, good." Irina blushed slightly. "Here she comes."

Mrs. Bugayev brought out a pot of hot tea, two cups, and a plateful of cookies. She placed them noisily on the round metal table and turned abruptly to go back in the house.

Of course. It was Mrs. Bugayev. She was the one Irina had meant was watching them.

"Thank you," Meg said to Mrs. Bugayev's retreating back. Knowing what she did now, Meg didn't really expect an answer and she didn't get one.

Do Russians always drink hot tea in 95-degree weather, Meg wondered? Iced tea with lots of sugar would have been better, but Meg was not about to ask for ice cubes and a glass.

"Do you like the garden? I need advice about flowers. Could you help?" Irina didn't wait for an answer. She stood up and led Meg through the tall fence gate to the front yard, where, at the end of the driveway, near the street, stood a large cement planter overflowing with green foliage and red blossoms.

"What are these?" Irina asked, bending over to inspect the plants.

"Oh, we have lots of those, too. They're geraniums. My mom likes them because they don't take much work," Meg said, joining Irina, who was now kneeling next to the planter and holding a blossom gently between her fingers.

"When we need to communicate secretly, the space under this planter will be our mailbox," Irina whispered without looking at Meg. "There is a message for you there now."

The planter stood on four short, fat legs leaving a small space between it and the ground.

Irina's words took Meg's breath away. Steady now, she told herself. Make the most famous detective in the world proud of his offspring. "Okay," she whispered.

"How often does your mother water her, uh, geraniums?" Irina spoke again in a normal tone. She stumbled only slightly over the word geranium.

"I don't know." Meg was still thinking about passing secret messages and found it hard to concentrate on geraniums. "But I think she feels the soil like this," she finally said, willing her excitement under control and moving slightly so that her crouched body would block the view from the house. She put one hand on top of the soil. She slipped the other under the planter and slowly slid out a piece of paper and squeezed it into her fist.

"Then when it's dry like this, she waters it." Meg rubbed the dry soil between her fingers and let it fall back into the planter.

"But why don't you come to dinner sometime and you can ask her yourself? She knows a lot about flowers." Meg felt Mrs. Bugayev's presence inside the house, and a tingle of pleasure ran through her body at the thought of deceiving her.

"Oh, dear. I don't know if I can do that." Irina, looking troubled, stood up and headed back to the patio.

Following her, Meg protested, "Why not?"

Irina sat down at the table again, folded her hands, and frowned at them. "I have to be very careful because of criminals and terrorists."

"What?" Meg thought she had misunderstood. She stuffed her fist with the note into her pocket as she sat down.

"Mrs. Bugayev is very concerned about our safety here in the United States because of all the criminals. I can't go places by myself."

"Tell her not to worry. *Nothing* ever happens around here. Only once, when old Mrs. Mc-Gillicutty's brooch was stolen. The police came and everything. I was helping them look for foot-prints in her backyard when she found it. Or rather the dry cleaners found it. She'd left it in her pocket."

"I don't know," Irina said doubtfully.

"She won't let you talk on the phone either. How

come?" Meg's curiosity overcame her guest manners.

"She says the phone is tapped. I'm not so sure — other than by the embassy, for our own protection, of course. What Mrs. Bugayev really worries about, I think, is that I will somehow really like American life and want to stay here. I cannot seem to convince her that is ridiculous."

Meg resisted the temptation to ask why it was ridiculous. She didn't want to trigger a political debate. She wanted Irina to relax, keep talking. Irina had already divulged important information. So the Lysikovs' phone was tapped — by the Soviet embassy! Maybe that was why the number was available through directory assistance. Traitors could find it and call in secrets, and the Soviets would record every word. A few things were beginning to fit together.

"Well, there probably won't be any criminals or terrorists at my house," Meg said, trying to lighten the conversation, to get Irina to relax and say more. "Except my little sister, Dorie. She's a closet terrorist."

"Your sister?" Irina's eyes widened.

"No. It's a joke. She's always taking stuff from my closet and trying it on and then leaving it in her closet." Meg wanted to reassure Irina, who looked genuinely shocked. "It's just a joke," Meg said again with emphasis.

"Yes. A joke," Irina repeated. She started to

smile. "She terrorizes your closet." Irina actually came close to laughing. "A little sister who is a terrorist."

Meg grinned, although it didn't seem to her the joke was *that* funny. For just a moment, as they exchanged smiles, Meg wondered what Irina was really like. There was something so serious and so sad about her. Maybe being the daughter of a spy had a downside. Mr. Lysikov didn't seem to be home very often. His car was hardly ever in the driveway, an inconvenience for Meg, who would have preferred spending time at Irina's house with Mr. Lysikov in it. For Irina, who didn't get to go to any secret rendezvous, it would make him just an ordinary, run-of-the-mill, very busy father.

"In Moscow, we don't worry about criminals. We can walk on the streets day or night."

Danger signals sounded in Meg's head. Was this the opening line to another lecture on the merits of Soviet life and the demerits of the good old U.S.A.? She quickly reviewed her own ammunition, but then, luckily, didn't have to use it. Irina went on quietly to tell Meg about winter walks with her father beneath dimly lit streetlamps with snow crunching under her thick boots.

As Irina talked, she sat on the edge of her chair and leaned over the table to get closer to Meg. She nibbled on the edge of a cookie. It was interesting information, but not relevant to Meg's case.

In fact, Irina sounded homesick. The thought of crunching snow was beginning to sound good to Meg, too. She might have to spend the rest of her life as a liquid if she didn't get into some air-conditioning.

"Do you have youth groups here? We do at home. I was going to be leader of my cell, but we came here."

"We have clubs, French club and Spanish club, and drama, stuff like that."

"I'll show you something. Wait just a minute, please."

While Irina was in the house, Meg assessed the situation. First, she took a professional point of view and congratulated herself on her discovery of the tapped phone. It had made the visit worthwhile. And, then, on a more personal level, it was possible that Irina might turn out okay. She was a lot more serious than Kathy and not funny, really, at all like Kathy, but she *did* want to pass secret notes, and that was an important sign of strong character.

Irina returned carrying a green velvet box with a gold seal on the top. It was as large as Meg's jewelry box, which was currently filled with her bottlecap collection.

"This is my badge collection," Irina said. She opened the box.

The sight stunned Meg. The box was filled to the top with medals and badges. Gold medallions and silver pins sparkled in the sunshine. A cloth-covered pin was striped blue and yellow and purple and red. It could have belonged to a general, somebody important who probably had to die to deserve it.

"Wow," Meg said, marveling at the collection. "How d'ya get these?"

"From different places at home. Each town in the Soviet Union has a pin. My father gets them when he travels. This one's from Moscow." Irina carefully extricated a shiny gold medal as large as her palm, a hammer and sickle in the center on a filigree background, and eight long points emerging from the center.

"This collection was my mother's. She loved the motherland so — and served it well. Now it's mine."

"It's like a treasure chest! You are *really* lucky," Meg said, saying the first thing that came into her head. Then she heard what she'd said and wished she hadn't because, of course, Irina wasn't really lucky at all. Having your mother die was probably the worst luck a kid could have.

Irina just nodded. "I have two of these," Irina said, picking out a gold pin the size of a quarter and handing it to Meg. It was square, with a white design and red background trimmed in gold. A red star, its tails falling gracefully behind it, rose high above five adjoining rings.

"What's it for?"

"It's from the Olympic Games in 1980. They were in Moscow. I was little at the time, but I remember it very well. We all went, my father, my mother, and I." Irina touched first one side of her collar, then the other, as though she might feel something still pinned there. Then she smiled. "Perhaps you have badges, too."

"Yeah. A few." It would be embarrassing to show Irina her collection. Meg had three Brownie Scout merit badges and lots of tin pins she'd collected on vacation. But even her oldest, and the one probably worth the most — an "I like Ike" campaign button she'd talked her father into giving up — was no rival to anything Irina had.

Meg fingered the Olympic pin. It was the most beautiful she had ever seen, far more impressive than a mere piece of jewelry. And it was heavy. "Is it real gold?"

Irina hesitated only a moment. "Yes."

Meg quickly gave it back. She had nothing that was real gold.

"I read in a book once that teenagers here sometimes have sleeping parties where nobody sleeps," Irina said as she rearranged the contents of her box and finally closed the lid.

It took Meg a minute to figure out what Irina was talking about. "Oh, slumber parties," she finally answered. "You don't have to be a teenager.

You just have a friend or a bunch of friends over to spend the night." Meg wanted to make up for the deficiency of her own badge collection. "I had my first friend over when I was eight." It might sound boastful, but it was the truth.

Irina suddenly stiffened. "I'll let you know what my father says about dinner at your house," she said formally.

Meg followed Irina's gaze and saw Mrs. Bugayev at the back door, holding the screen door open. It was something more than a hint. Time to go.

Irina stood up and Meg followed her lead. Mrs. Bugayev must have been watching from the kitchen window, Meg guessed. Could she have heard them talking, guessed about the secret note she had in her pocket? Meg could not bring herself to meet the eyes of the frowning Mrs. Bugayev, but she did have an inspired idea.

"Hey, Irina," she said as she walked through the house to the front door. "If you want, I'll put some special fertilizer my mom has on those geraniums of yours."

"Thank you very much," Irina said formally while nodding enthusiastically from behind Mrs. Bugayev's back.

Meg hurried across the street and up to her room. She pulled Irina's note from her pocket and scribbled over the crumpled paper with her developer pen.

Mrs. Bugayev is very old-fashioned. I want her to stop worrying about me. I talked about the United States when you first came over because I knew she was listening and I thought it would make her worry less. She thinks capitalists, and especially Americans, are immoral, and she does not want us to be friends. I called my father after you phoned today and he told her to let you come. I think it made her angry. She does not like you, but I like you very much.

Irina

Meg read the note three times. It was odd to think someone so strongly disapproved of her. She called her mother to see what night would be best for Irina to come to dinner. Her mother's kind voice, though rushed, reassured her. There was really no reason a normal adult should disapprove of her.

She took out her ghostwriter.

Dear Irina,

I think Mrs. Bugayev is a little mixed-up. Economics has nothing to do with friendship. It's sort of like going to different churches. My best friend Kathy is a Catholic and she believes in the Pope.

*I am a Methodist and I don't. But we
hardly ever talk about the Pope. In fact,
I can't remember ever talking about the
Pope. So it doesn't affect our friendship
one little bit. Maybe if you and I hang
around together for a while, Mrs. Bugayev will get used to me and forget I'm
a capitalist. (I might not even be a real
capitalist yet since I don't have a job.)
If your dad says you can, please come
to dinner on Tuesday at 6 P.M.*

*Your friend,
Meg*

She rushed to the garden shed, grabbed the
small bag of fertilizer, raced across the street,
poured a little on the geraniums, feigned a close
inspection of the plant while pushing her note
under the planter, and ran back home. She'd felt
she was being watched and was both relieved and
annoyed when she saw a glimpse of Dorie's head
disappear behind the upstairs bathroom curtain.

Back in her house and breathing hard, Meg
yelled up the stairs, "Dorie, I saw you. Stop
spying on me." There was no answer, only the
sound of pounding that Meg followed into the
kitchen. She didn't want to forget to tell Celia
that Irina might be coming for dinner the following Tuesday.

"That will be nice, *niña*. What would you like to have?" Celia said as she pounded chicken and placed it in a bowl of marinade.

Niña. The familiar Spanish word was comforting. It was what Celia had called her ever since she was little.

"Chocolate cake. And, Celia, I can peel the potatoes if you want, before I set the table," Meg offered. She needed to think about Mrs. Bugayev, who didn't even know her but disliked her anyway, and she wanted to do it in the kitchen working next to Celia.

8

Irina arrived for dinner on Tuesday in brand-new blue jeans, a floppy sweatshirt with HARVARD written across the front, and a new pair of Nike tennis shoes with no socks.

She may not like America, but she likes American clothes, Meg thought. Of course, no American kid in her right mind would wear a sweatshirt in this weather. She's just lucky we have air-conditioning.

"Hi, I'm Dorie. Can I ask you a question?" Dorie had screeched to a halt in front of Irina.

"Hello, Dorie," Irina said softly. "I have heard many things about you." She grinned at Meg in a knowing way.

"How come you're scared of lunch boxes?" The question burst from Dorie's mouth and then she stood, hands at her sides, waiting patiently for an answer.

It was clear Irina had no idea what Dorie was

68

talking about. So much had happened since, it even took Meg a minute to figure it out.

"She means the first day we met. At the carnival last month. You wouldn't talk to me and you looked scared," Meg explained. "Remember, I wanted to trade you a lunch box?"

"Oh, yes, of course. That was only a few weeks ago, but it seems so much longer. It was my second day here, and I wanted to see the neighborhood where I would be living. I went in one of the embassy cars and, when I saw the fair, I just had to get out to take a look. I had a very kind driver and he said as long as I didn't speak to anyone, I could go see." Irina turned to Meg. "You were the first American to speak to me. You see, I couldn't talk. I'd promised."

"So you're not afraid of lunch boxes?" Dorie asked.

"No, of course not." Irina laughed.

Dorie frowned at Meg. "You were wrong. She's *not* afraid of lunch boxes." Then she turned on her heels and headed back toward the basement playroom.

Meg shrugged and shook her head. "C'mon up to my room, Irina. Mom's still cooking."

"What did Dorie mean?" Irina asked, following Meg up the stairs.

"Oh, Dorie's just glad when I'm wrong about something. She's been like that lately. It's some kind of phase she's going through." Meg wanted to change the subject. "I'm glad your dad let you come," she said as Irina sat down primly on the bed, both feet on the floor. Meg wondered what they would talk about all evening.

"He said it was okay." Irina emphasized "okay" and grinned. She was in a festive mood.

"What did Mrs. B say?" Meg gave in to the temptation to ask the obvious question and, in the process, shortened the housekeeper's name. It gave her a sense of control over the woman. Besides, she wasn't sure she could pronounce Bugayev.

"I told her about old Mrs. McGillicutty's brooch, but she still did not want me to come. I must remember she is always trying to protect me." Irina's festive mood evaporated. She slumped on the bed, staring at her new tennis shoes.

Meg, feeling somehow responsible, wanted to cheer her up. "Hey, I think we can use these walkie-talkies!" she said, opening her desk drawer and pulling out two black plastic rectangles with red buttons on the front and red antennae sticking out.

"They let you have these?" Irina looked surprised. She held the one Meg had given her with two hands, cradling it as though it were a precious doll.

"Sure. They'll probably work from across the street. I'll get some new batteries from Dad, and you can take one home with you. It'll be fun," Meg said. It would be fun, all right, to talk on the walkie-talkies after dark when Meg's parents thought she was asleep. She and Kathy had tried it once, but Kathy lived too far away.

"Can we do it tonight?" Irina whispered. Her eyes were bright, and her grin had returned and spread almost the width of her narrow face. She liked the idea as much as Meg did.

Meg nodded. She stopped worrying about how she was going to entertain Irina all evening. The two of them really did like the same things.

"Can I look in your closet?" Irina asked.

"Sure," Meg replied. She liked to look in other kids' closets, too. She and Kathy did it all the time; in fact, sometimes they traded clothes. Meg hadn't seen Irina wear any clothes Meg wanted to trade, but she didn't mind Irina looking.

When Meg opened her closet door, videotapes came crashing from the top shelf onto the floor, missing her head by inches. She'd shoved them there in a hurried attempt to clean her room before Irina's arrival.

"You have a movie machine?" Irina bent to pick up the plastic boxes and read the titles.

"Yeah, a VCR. These are just some old videos I got as presents."

"*Gone With the Wind,*" Irina read aloud. "I read that book in Moscow. Can we watch this?"

"Sure, after dinner. Kathy and I watch it all the time."

"You have so many clothes, too." Irina seemed to be talking to herself as she turned to the closet. *Gone With the Wind* in one hand, she flipped slowly through the hangers with the other.

"In the last fifty years, the Soviet Union has gone from the most backward country in Europe to a leader of the world." Irina's voice was slightly muffled, since she was talking into the closet, but her words were as clear as the howl of a hurricane, and just as devastating, to Meg. "Now we are working toward a perfect society where we will have all the consumer goods we want without giving up our spiritual lives."

Uh-oh, trouble. Meg didn't want to talk about countries, or societies, or spiritual life. She just wanted to have fun. Maybe, hope against hope, this was just a temporary setback.

"We won't have social classes. Like your housekeeper. She would be equal to your President."

Get out the placards. Woman the barricades. Celia's already better than any president, Meg retorted silently. It had to be silent because Irina had launched into a long monologue about something called "sozialnost." She even spelled it for Meg. It sounded a lot like the Brownie Scout code.

Meg glared at Irina from her cross-legged position in the middle of the shaggy white rug. Irina would pull a hanger out of the closet and put the dress or skirt or blouse on it up to herself in the mirror, put it back, and quickly pull out another, talking the whole time in an earnest tone. It really was too much for Meg. She considered herself, under ordinary circumstances, a generous and forgiving hostess. But Irina had gone too far. One minute, a regular kid. The next, a missionary. Irina was trying to convert her to communism in her own bedroom. While checking out her clothes.

Meg cleared her throat. Just as she was about to say that it was too bad kids in the Soviet Union were not allowed to wear the kind of sequined T-shirt Irina was admiring that very minute, Meg's mother called them to dinner.

As they all settled in around the kitchen table, Mrs. Donovan asked Irina what most surprised her about the United States.

"The giant grocery store," Irina replied without hesitation.

"Oh, yes. It's big, isn't it?" Mrs. Donovan replied.

"It's bigger than my hometown," Mr. Donovan said and laughed at his own joke. Meg had heard it before.

"I was surprised to see a man with torn clothes and holes in his shoes shouting outside the store," Irina said. Mr. Donovan filled Irina's plate with chicken, mashed potatoes, and broccoli.

"Yes, it's sad to see," Mrs. Donovan answered. "Sometimes it's drugs or alcohol, sometimes mental illness — sometimes it's somebody just down on his luck."

"But nobody paid any attention to this man. They walked by him," Irina said, picking up a bite of broccoli with her fork.

"I guess we've gotten used to it somehow," Mr. Donovan admitted.

"It seems to me we could do a better job caring for these people. Surely we could build decent places for them — places where they could live," Mrs. Donovan said, more to Mr. Donovan than to Irina.

"They're rounding up the homeless in New York and putting them in shelters," said Mr. Donovan. "A lot of people are up in arms about it, and think the rights of the homeless are being violated."

No, no, no, Meg thought. Come on, Mom and Dad. Defend the way we do things here. Don't you know Irina is storing up ammunition? But her parents went on, ignoring her mental messages.

Meg couldn't stand it anymore. She broke in. "Frankly," she said, "I would rather live in a country where crazy people are on the streets than where sane people are put in mental institutions."

Mrs. Donovan's fork halted halfway between her plate and her mouth. She shot a warning look across the table at Meg. Dorie kept rubbing the condensation on her glass of milk, her mind far away. Irina ignored Meg's comment.

"I have one thing I would very much like to do while I am in your country," Irina said.

"What is that, honey?" Mrs. Donovan asked.

"I would like to speak about my country to a youth meeting," said Irina, her face glowing. "We are working toward a more democratic and just society, and we have a new policy of *glasnost* — openness. Everything will be changing, getting better and better. And we want to be friends with every country in the world, especially the United States."

There was a long silence around the Donovan table.

"Sounds like you'll need a stepladder to get home," Meg spoke into her dinner.

Irina smiled uncertainly at Mr. and Mrs. Donovan.

" 'Cause it's so close to heaven, you know," Meg said sweetly to Irina, feeling her mother's disapproval.

Irina relaxed and nodded. Meg did not look at her mother.

"Irina, that is a lovely idea. And it takes quite a bit of spunk," Mrs. Donovan said with determination. "Meg, aren't there some events coming up? I'm sure some of your friends would love to hear Irina talk about the Soviet Union."

There is no chance any of my friends would like to hear one word from Irina about the Soviet Union, Meg thought, but she didn't say it. She chewed vigorously, stalling for time. After all, she couldn't talk with a full mouth.

Dorie came out of her daydream. "There's that teen dance at the pool every Friday night," she said excitedly. "She could make a speech."

Meg, the bite thoroughly chewed, could not swallow it. She saw a long and lonely future in which she was known only as the girl who brought a Russian kid to talk about Soviet *glasnost* at the Friday-night pool dance.

"I have a better idea," Mr. Donovan said, clearing his throat. "Why don't you girls come to the hearing on Friday? The Secretary of State is testifying about the upcoming U.S.-Soviet summit. You won't be able to speak, Irina, but it might be better to wait until September to do that. I'm sure a number of the civics classes in the area would consider it an honor to have you as a guest speaker."

"That sounds splendid, Mr. Donovan."

Meg closed her eyes and swallowed. Thanks to her father, she'd been saved from a bleak and lonesome future. Now all she had to do was talk Irina out of going to the hearing.

"It won't be so splendid," Meg told Irina after dinner. "In fact, hearings are the most boring things on earth. Even my dad says so. They have to pay him to go. There's no reason to sit there for free." Meg had double-checked to make sure her father was out of earshot.

"Your father says it is about the summit," Irina said. "Will they serve cake?"

"It's not a party. It's a hearing. Senators ask long, boring questions, and witnesses give long, boring answers."

"I want to hear about the summit," Irina said stubbornly.

"You won't like it," Meg warned, feeling stubborn herself.

They spent the rest of the evening watching *Gone With the Wind* in the basement playroom. Irina lay on the carpet, her head on a pillow Dorie had given her, and listened to every word. Dorie lay right beside Irina, pretending to understand everything that was going on. In fact, Dorie was obnoxious. She *oohed* and *aahed* every time Rhett Butler appeared.

Meg and Kathy usually played Clue or Scrabble or Concentration when they watched *Gone With the Wind*. Tonight, she had no partner so she tried putting together a jigsaw puzzle by herself, gave it up, and then turned to a book and gave that up. In the end, she watched *Gone With the Wind* while leafing through Dorie's comic collection.

Finally, it was time for Irina to go home. Just as she was leaving, Irina remembered the walkie-talkie. As Meg's father found new batteries, Meg gave Irina a lesson on how to use a walkie-talkie. Push this button to call, this button to talk, this button to listen. Meg wondered the whole time which of the two Irinas would be using it. Would it be the warm and friendly one who wrote secret notes? Or would the Communist missionary use it to broadcast political propaganda?

Then, just as Irina was about to go out the door, walkie-talkie in hand, she leaned toward Meg to whisper something. "Just a small message," she said conspiratorially and nodded toward her house across the street.

"I'm gonna walk Irina home," Meg announced aloud to her parents, as she and Irina walked out the door.

"I really like your family. Thank you for inviting me to dinner," Irina said quietly as they walked across the street.

"Sure." It had not been an evening of belly laughs. She'd thought Irina might be a good substitute for Kathy, at least until Kathy got back from California. But tonight had gone sour. First, there was Irina's political lecture. It had not been for Mrs. Bugayev's benefit this time. Then there was Irina's determination to address youth groups. It bordered on the fanatic. And then with *Gone With the Wind*, Irina had just watched it, glued.

They stopped at the planter and Meg leaned over to feel the soil. It was damp.

"Needs watering," Meg said, ignoring the soggy soil and nodding toward the green hose wound tightly around its large spool next to the house.

The two struggled with the hose, watered the geraniums, and rewound the hose. In the process,

Meg managed to slip her hand under the planter and bring out a small bit of tissue paper crumpled into a ball.

" 'Night, Irina. See ya later."

Back in her room, before Meg had completely opened it, a small object dropped out of the paper and tumbled onto the shag rug. It was the pin from the Moscow Olympics, one of Irina's favorites from her badge collection, and it was gold. Meg scribbled on both sides of the tissue paper with her developer pen. There was no message.

9

It was morning and Meg was checking the value of gold in the financial section of the *Washington Post*. That done, she figured her new gold pin was worth over two hundred dollars. The knowledge quickly softened Meg's opinion of Irina from the night before. Maybe she was being too hard on her. Maybe she ought to give Irina another chance.

"Telephone, *niña*."

"Hello. Would you like to come to my house?" It was Irina. Her voice sounded far away. Maybe that was because she knew she was being recorded. But she *was* using the phone. Hurrah for the good guys. Mrs. Bugayev had been foiled again.

Meg pulled the telephone extension cord to its limit, straining to look out the dining room window from the kitchen. Mr. Lysikov's car was not in the driveway. Meg did not want to spend the day at Irina's house. "It's so hot. Why don't we go to the pool? You can come as my guest."

"I must speak to my father," Irina said and hung up. She was back to Meg in five minutes.

"I can go!" Irina's voice was now strong and confident.

"Meet you in front in ten minutes. We'll walk."

Meg had gone to the neighborhood pool a week earlier. Nobody had been there, except little kids and their mothers. She'd tried reading for an hour in one of the lounge chairs. She hadn't taken a swim. She hadn't even taken off her terrycloth robe. It had made her so lonesome for Kathy, she'd had no thought about going back until now.

The swimming pool was not at all fancy like a country club. It was cut out of the neighborhood in an irregular fashion, as though by a giant three-year-old. Huge trees towered above it, and shrubs ran alongside the corrugated fence. An unpaved lane skirted one side, leading to a small parking lot behind the pool. Meg had been swimming there all her life.

Today, as Meg and Irina entered the swimming pool gate, a girl in a royal blue tank suit waved at them from behind the diving boards across the pool. Meg waved back.

"Lacey Darcy," Meg said, in explanation to Irina, as she paid the guest fee and then led Irina into the small dressing and shower area.

"She is a friend?" Irina asked.

"Yeah." It was not a lie. Lacey Darcy *was* Meg's friend. In fact, Lacey Darcy was everyone's friend. She seemed to collect friends like Meg collected slides of insect parts. In Meg's opinion, she even labeled and filed them in categories. Meg was sure it was Lacey who had come up with "the Human Library."

Meg had worn her suit under her shirt and jeans and was waiting outside the dressing room when Irina emerged. Irina wore a turquoise suit with small white dots. It had thin straps, a built-in bra, and a little ruffled skirt around the hips. Meg remembered a picture of her mother in an old photo album. It was taken when she was a teenager, and she'd had on a bathing suit a lot like Irina's. Meg ordinarily did not take much notice of clothes, but in this case, Irina's suit was hard to ignore.

Irina was staring at Meg's suit, a lavender tank suit with a light blue and darker blue stripe running diagonally from hip to under her arm. Meg's new gold pin, attached just below one of the straps, sparkled in the sunlight.

"You look swell," Irina said.

"You look okay, too," Meg said, trying to sound reassuring. She didn't want to tell Irina that both "swell" and Irina's swimming suit had been obsolete for decades.

"Hey, Meg, over here!" Lacey was waving and shouting. She sat between two other girls, their brightly colored beach towels spread neatly under them.

If Kathy had been there, she would have flopped down first, Meg on the outside. But, today, Meg laid her towel next to Peggy's, and Irina sat on the outside.

"Irina, this is Lacey, Peggy, and that's Cass, over there. This is Irina from the Soviet Union. She's moved in across the street." Meg made the introductions as she spread her towel and straightened the corners to lie flat.

"Wow. A real Communist! Hi!" Cass giggled behind one hand and waved limply with the other toward Irina.

"It's wonderful to meet you," Lacey said, smiling broadly. "Will you be going to the junior high?"

"No, I must go to the embassy school," Irina said, nodding back.

"Too bad," Lacey said and turned to watch one of the boys doing a cannonball from the high dive. Meg figured Lacey had already lost interest in Irina as a collector's item.

"How do you like America?" Peggy asked.

Meg waited for Irina's lecture to begin.

"I like it very much," Irina said. And then nothing more. Meg imagined the missionary Irina still home asleep while the friendly one sat here beside her at the pool.

"You must bring Irina to Sally's Friday night."

Lacey still faced the pool. "What are you wearing? We're thinking about wearing dresses."

"To Sally's? I haven't been invited." It was not the sort of announcement Meg enjoyed making. Not that she was surprised she wasn't invited. She hardly knew Sally. Sally was not one of Lacey's "regulars." For that matter, neither was Meg. No, if Meg were going to have a party, she would want Lacey to come, no doubt about that, but she wouldn't even think of Sally.

"Oh, Meg. I'm sorry. I shouldn't have mentioned it. I just assumed you'd be going. It'll probably be boring. Sally's sort of a nerd." Lacey looked genuinely distressed.

Lacey's sympathy made it worse. As though there really were something she'd be missing. "Doesn't matter. I'm already busy."

"That's an awesome pin," Cass offered.

"Yeah, it's real gold. Irina gave it to me." Meg detached it from her suit and handed it over for inspection.

Meg took a second to smile at Irina, who was blushing a deep red, as the girls *oohed* and *aahed* at the pin.

Lacey handed it back. "It's such a beautiful present, Irina. You're really lucky, Meg." Lacey had conferred her blessing.

At that moment, four wet boys appeared dripping beside the girls' towels, Kenny Davis towering above them. A boy took the arm of each of the other three girls and pulled them, squealing and giggling, toward the pool.

"How 'bout a swim, Meg?" Jack, shiny as an eel, teeth bright white in the sun, grabbed Meg's hand and tugged hard.

"As though I've got a choice." Meg laughed and offered little resistance. "Hey, you've got to get Irina, too. Irina, this is Jack." Meg shouted the introduction just as she careened head first into the pool.

They spent five hours at the pool. Hot dogs for lunch, games of cards on the beach towels, races with the boys, clowning off the high dive. It was a perfect day. Even Irina relaxed and seemed to have fun. She taught them all how to do swan dives.

"What is a nerd?" Irina asked as they walked home. The road smelled of tar and glistened in the heat. Their tennis shoes stuck to the surface, protesting noisily after every step.

"It's somebody you don't wanna be," Meg said. "It's like having the plague."

"A sick person?"

"No, not really." She tried again. "It's sort of an intellectual kid who can't get their head out of a book to see what's going on."

"Oh. But your friends are going to a party at a nerd's house."

"Yeah," Meg said. "That's different." Meg was not sure how to explain so Irina could understand.

She tried to make it simple. "It's like this. At parties, there's lots of good food, and the boys come and you play fun games and dance and stuff. So, even if it's at a nerd's house, it's worth going."

Irina still looked mystified. "And the girl Lacey. Is she your leader?"

Now Irina was beginning to understand a little social dynamics. "My best friend and I have Lacey all figured out." This was something Meg could explain with her eyes closed. "We figure she's already running for homecoming queen — that's when everybody votes for the most popular girl in senior high school. She's nice to everybody, sort of charms all the jealousy out. She's especially sweet to any girl who might be competition, tries to bring her in, make her a member of the court before she gets ideas about being queen herself."

Irina was shaking her head. "It is very difficult for me." She brightened. "So she has trapped that boy, the one who looks like the star in your movie, *Gone With the Wind*. He will be king?"

Irina *had* understood about Lacey Darcy. Just like Kathy. Completely.

Meg threw her towel in the air and caught it with one hand. "Whoopee! You're okay, Irina." And she meant it.

10

Meg did not see Irina again until Friday, the day of the hearing. The day before, she had found a note under the geranium planter:

Thank you for taking me to the pool. You are a little different from your friends. You do not giggle. I think this is very good. Do you think my speech has an accent?

Irina

Meg had had to think about Irina's message for a while before replying. She spent a little time watching herself giggle in front of a mirror. It *did* look unnatural. But, then, she couldn't think of anything even remotely funny when she looked in the mirror. So the experiment probably wasn't valid, at least from a scientific point of view. Irina had made an interesting observation though, and

Meg liked it, even if it could not be proven absolutely one hundred percent true.

> *Dear Irina,*
>
> *It is true that I have a more sophisticated sense of humor than many of my friends. I don't write this to brag in any way, just to explain to you why I don't giggle. You do have an accent, but so do a lot of other people here in D.C. Celia does, and a Korean girl in my music class does, and, so do the Pakistanis who live at the end of the block. Also people who live in different parts of the U.S. It's no big deal.*
>
> *Meg*

The day of the hearing, Mr. Lysikov delivered Irina to the Donovans' front door. Meg, standing behind her father, listened to the exchange. Irina was to be taken home by an embassy limousine that would pick her up at the Senate steps after the hearing. Mr. Lysikov was exceedingly grateful to Mr. Donovan for the opportunity he was providing Irina. It should be an instructive day. The two shook hands in a warm and friendly way. And that was it.

Meg had not yet had a chance to tell her dad about the Lysikovs' tapped phone. She knew he wouldn't consider it conclusive evidence. But she'd tell him anyway. She wanted to keep him on his guard.

The three drove to the Capitol in traffic so thick and slow, it would have been faster to ride bikes. To avoid heavy traffic, Mr. Donovan tried a route that took them by the White House. There, they had had to wait as several hundred demonstrators crossed Pennsylvania Avenue on their way to chant and march in front of the White House. Meg's father groaned and leaned forward in his seat over the wheel, as though any forward movement, no matter how small, would ease his tension.

"What are they doing? Will they be arrested?" Irina asked, amazement in her voice.

"They're trying to get the government to tighten emissions standards for automobiles. And, no, they won't get arrested. But we are thinking of passing a law to deny free speech during rush hour — as a clean air measure to cut down on noxious fumes," Mr. Donovan responded grimly.

Meg knew her father's comment was meant to be a joke. She also knew it had passed right by Irina. An appreciation for sick humor was not among Irina's character traits.

"The President's house is not so big." Irina leaned out the window, stretching her neck to get a good view of the White House.

"No, it's not." Meg's father sat back again. "You see, we didn't want any president taking on the power or even the trappings of a king. . . ." And so the lecture began. Meg, in the backseat, was glad her father had something to distract him from the fact that he was probably going to be late for work. She stared at Irina's long braid, wondering whether Irina left it braided for several days at a time, or whether she had to undo it every night and redo it every morning.

Meg awoke from her reverie to point out the great beige FBI building they were passing on the left. She'd be working there someday.

"Oh, dear, it looks upside down. Is the CIA there, too?" Irina asked. To Meg's ears, her voice had the slightest shiver of fear in it.

"No. The CIA's out in Virginia. And the FBI isn't scary at all. It's the best tour in town . . . only on weekdays, never on weekends. You get to shoot a real gun and see how they match fingerprints. They'll even take your fingerprints if you want. You'd love it."

"What's that ahead?" Irina asked. She showed no interest in having her fingerprints taken. Meg was disappointed at first. The FBI had three sets of Meg's fingerprints, six-year-old prints, eight-year-old prints, and then the ones they'd taken last year when she was ten. On reflection, Meg figured Irina's reluctance was probably natural given her family history.

Meg looked beyond Irina's shoulder at the wide avenue lined by trees and large buildings. The scene formed a frame for the large and graceful Capitol building on the hill ahead, its great, white dome shimmering in the sun. "It's the Capitol where they have the best fireworks on the Fourth of July. Can we take Irina, Dad?"

"Sure. The Capitol also has a secondary function that Irina might be interested in. It's the home of our parliament, Irina. The Senate sits there on the left — that's where you'll be today in one of the committee rooms. And the House of Representatives sits over there on the right. . . ."

Meg had heard it all before so she barely listened. But she did feel a rush of happiness, looking at the Capitol. It had to do with the upcoming fireworks, for sure. But there was something else, too, something less explainable. The building looked so strong, so safe, so self-assured against the blue sky. Somehow she was seeing it fresh and new, maybe because Irina was seeing it for the first time, and some of that newness had rubbed off on Meg. Normally Meg took all the famous monuments and buildings for granted. But, for a fleeting moment, she thought how special a place Washington, D.C., is to live.

Once in the Senate Dirksen Building, Mr. Donovan rushed the girls through the security gates, up the stairs, and through the noisy and frenetic anteroom into the hearing room. There he left them.

They finally found some chairs that were not

marked "reserved" near the back of the huge room.

"I tried to call you on the walkie-talkie last night," Meg whispered as they sat down. The high ceilings, the formal decor, and the expectant hush of the room made her want to whisper, even though the doors had not yet been opened and there was no one to overhear. The Capitol Hill guards stood stiffly far away by the door, and the television technicians were chatting as they adjusted their cameras and lights at the front of the room.

Irina whispered back, "I know. I heard it beeping. I had to put it under my mattress so Mrs. Bugayev could not hear. She was in her room working. I couldn't talk." She was looking wide-eyed around the room.

Twenty minutes later, the room was full. Sitting back with Meg and Irina were tourists in shorts and "I love D.C." T-shirts, trying to keep wiggly children under control. In front of them sat several rows of diplomats wearing dark suits or navy blue dresses. Journalists, dressed more colorfully, most reading newspapers, lined two long tables on either side of the room. Several of the men had taken off their suit jackets and two wore bright red suspenders. The women wore pastels except for one who was wearing a white linen suit with a splashy orange scarf. Meg figured she was probably famous, though she didn't recognize her.

"This hearing will please come to order," the Chairman intoned from his seat at the dais. Meg could see only the back of the head of the Secretary of State and that of one of his advisors who had joined him at the witness table. Meg saw her father sitting behind the Chairman and she thought he winked at her, but he was so far away she couldn't be sure.

As the Secretary began his testimony, the Chairman buried his head in some papers and began to write intermittently. Another Senator was reading, and a third was having an intense conversation with an assistant squatting on the floor beside her chair. Even Mr. Donovan was shuffling papers on his lap.

"No one is listening to the Secretary of State," Irina whispered to Meg.

"That's right. It's not a listening. It's a hearing," Meg whispered back solemnly.

Irina looked puzzled but nodded her head as though she understood and turned her attention back to the Secretary's testimony.

The hearing was just as boring as Meg had expected. The Secretary droned on, and the Senators asked long, drawn-out questions that deserved periods instead of question marks.

Then, Senator Scannon's turn rolled around.

Meg's father was known to complain about Senator Scannon. "Loose cannon" and "unguided missile" were the names associated with the Senator, at least in the Donovan household. "Now about this glassnosed, or whatever the blamed thing is called, have you ever considered, Mr. Secretary, that it's a trick?"

"We measure Soviet actions, not words, Senator Scannon. That is not to say we don't appreciate Soviet efforts, which do appear real, to move toward a more open society," the Secretary replied evenly.

"They're buying time, lulling us into letting down our guard, romancin' Europe to weaken NATO. Are people over at the State Department falling for this Russian eyewash, Mr. Secretary?"

Irina stiffened. Meg sat forward on the edge of her chair. Now this was getting a little more interesting. She could use a few good arguments. The missionary Irina had a way of emerging unexpectedly, and Meg was in need of ammunition to beat her back.

"The TV cameras are still on. Can't the Chairman get them turned off? Or at least make him stop saying those things?" Irina whispered worriedly to Meg.

"Nope. The Chairman doesn't have any control over anybody."

"But this will confuse people watching." Irina's voice sounded strained.

Meg shrugged. "It's a free country." Then, feeling her remark might have been a little callous, she stole a look at Irina.

Irina was twisting a Kleenex in her hands, her eyebrows knit together, and her mouth twisted to the side. She was taking this much too seriously, probably more seriously than anybody else in the room, or in the whole United States for that matter, Meg thought.

Still, Meg couldn't help but feel sympathy. "Look, Irina, he's only one Senator. There are a hundred, and they all think differently."

Two people in front of them turned around. Meg couldn't tell whether the signal to be quiet was directed at them or a nearby child who was choo-chooing his invisible train at a loud and dangerous speed. The parents shushed the child, and Meg and Irina didn't say another word until the end of the hearing.

Finally, the Secretary finished answering all the questions and the hearing adjourned. As the Secretary walked out, his assistant followed him carrying a briefcase.

"Nobody, not even him," Irina said, nodding toward the Secretary of State, "understands what is going on in my country."

Meg stood on her tiptoes, straining to see the

two men over the heads of the crowd. "Yeah, that's why we gotta talk, I guess," she said distractedly. That man with the Secretary looked familiar. Then it came to her.

Meg rushed Irina to the waiting limousine, hardly saying good-bye to her. It took her another ten minutes to find her father back in the hearing room.

"Dad, that man, he's the one at the East Building." Meg was breathless. The words were a whisper.

"Where's Irina?" Mr. Donovan looked anxiously around the emptying room.

"In the limousine. She's okay." After her father was satisfied that Irina was safe, it was a struggle to get his full attention again. He seemed to be thinking about everything except what Meg was saying.

"The Secretary's assistant, Dad. He was the one Mr. Lysikov was talking to in the East Wing." This time she tugged on his sleeve as she said it.

"Oh, honey, you've got him mixed up with somebody else," her father said, now hurrying down the corridor to his office. "He's one of our top arms control negotiators. He sees the Soviets every day across the negotiating table. No need for him to see them secretly."

Meg stopped in the corridor, so he had to stop, too. "Dad, this is a one hundred percent, absolute, certain identification." She said it slowly, firmly.

Her father looked at her intently, his head cocked to one side. He was making up his mind. "Then we'd better tell the FBI," he said quietly.

He rushed into his office, Meg close behind, shut the door, and picked up the phone.

11

That night, Meg lay in her bed thinking about the FBI. She would do everything she could to help them. Sherlock Holmes always cooperated with Scotland Yard. He even let them take the credit when it was actually he who had solved the case. Meg was prepared to be equally generous to the Federal Bureau of Investigation.

Her planning was interrupted by the muffled sound of beeping. She slowly got out of bed so that her parents downstairs would not hear her, and she quietly opened a drawer to pull out her walkie-talkie.

She had never gotten a night call. In fact, she had only used her walkie-talkie in the backyard and on hikes with her parents. Now, with just those few beeps, the former toy had been transformed into a clandestine communications device.

She tried to contain her excitement as she crawled back into bed and pulled her sheets and blanket over her head. She turned it on and pressed the receiver button. She heard static. She beeped, pressed the receiver button again, and turned up the volume. Louder static.

She came out from under the covers, remembered the window was closed because of the air-conditioning, opened it as quietly as possible, and put the walkie-talkie up to the screen.

"Are you there, Meg?" The voice was faint and almost drowned out by static. But it was a voice. Meg had to take a deep breath before she could respond.

"Yes. I am here. Over." Meg tried to sound professional. She willed her Sherlock Holmes blood to calm her heartbeat.

"I would like to have a sleeping party," the voice came again.

Meg was not sure she was ready for a sleepover with Irina. If she'd had to rate the night Irina came to dinner on a social scale from "one-rolling in the aisles hilarious" to "ten-stifling as a stuffy coffin," she would have given it a "nine." When Irina went into her missionary mode, she was as dry as the apple cores Meg sometimes found under her bed. On the other hand, Irina could be fun when she was sending secret messages or teaching Meg how to swan dive or, now, talking on the walkie-talkie.

"Where? Over," Meg replied, stalling for time.

99

"At your house," came the expected answer. It was hardly audible through the static, and Meg had to turn up the volume again.

Meg calculated the number of hours Irina would be at her house. Probably about sixteen, only eight of which would be sleeping. Maybe she could handle the other eight, take control of them, get Irina to assist in developing a new code or even practice Morse code on the walkie-talkie beepers until they got it right.

"Okay. Maybe tomorrow night. I'll ask my parents. Over."

There was no response. She pressed the receiver button until her thumb ached. She pressed the beeper. Nothing.

Meg started as a small, shadowy figure appeared at her bedroom door. A paper airplane flew by Meg's ear.

"Dorie, what are you doing?" Meg whispered.

"It's a secret message from Russia," Dorie whispered back, using her imitation robot voice.

"IIey, what's going on up there?" Mr. Donovan's voice boomed up the stairway.

Dorie scrambled back to her room. Meg lay there brooding. Dorie had found out about the secret messages! Dorie had never been able to keep a secret. Every year, well before Christmas, Dorie told Meg what present she'd bought for her. This past year, Dorie had told her in September what she was planning to buy for her in December.

Meg had to do something and quickly. Otherwise Celia, her parents, and even the letter carrier would probably know about the secret hiding place.

Meg tiptoed into Dorie's room. "Dorie, I gotta talk to you."

Dorie sat up quickly in bed. Meg could just see the outline of Dorie's white nightshirt as Meg sat gently on the edge of the bed.

"About what?"

"About being my junior partner. You wanna be?"

"Yeah," Dorie whispered enthusiastically.

"I'm working on a case now, looking for a Soviet spy."

"I know. What can I do?" Dorie was now whispering so softly, Meg could hardly hear her.

"Nothing. Just keep quiet about everything I do. Including secret hiding places. Know what I mean?"

"Sure, but I want to do something. Like that time I told you to call directory assistance. Is that the sort of thing junior partners do?" Dorie was becoming insistent.

It was time for Meg to take a firm line. "They follow orders from senior partners. I'm the senior partner and I say you've gotta keep things secret or you're out of it. Understand?"

"Okay, partner, but sometime can you think of something for me to really do?"

"Sure. 'Night, Dorie." Meg tiptoed back to her own room, congratulating herself. Sometimes she was unexpectedly brilliant with Dorie, even now that her little sister was getting a little more difficult to manage.

Back in bed, Meg tried once more to communicate with Irina. This time she muffled the beeping with her pillow. Still no response. Finally she gave up, closed the window, and climbed back into bed. It was a long time before she fell asleep.

The next day was Saturday. Meg woke up unusually late and her first thought was Irina. Now that Mr. Lysikov was going to be picked up by the FBI, what was going to happen to her? He'd be put in jail or sent back to the Soviet Union. Then he'd probably have to go live in Siberia, and Irina would have to go with him. It seemed an undeserved fate for a kid brave enough to pass secret messages.

Thinking about it that way, Meg saw her self-assigned mission in a new light, as something that might have bad consequences for someone she knew and even, sort of, liked. It was only a whisper of guilt, but it took effort to brush it aside. She could not let sentiment deter her from protecting the whole United States, could she? Who ever heard of a softhearted sleuth? She squashed the guilt.

As she clumped heavily down the stairs, she could see her father crouched outside on the front stoop, preparing to sand the warped front screen door. He was feeling the bottom edge of the door with the tips of his fingers, his electric drill with the sander attachment held in his other hand like a weapon.

"Do you think the FBI will want to question me about Mr. Lysikov?" Meg asked through the screen.

"I don't know, honey. Probably not," Mr. Donovan replied and turned on the electric sander. The squeal pierced her brain.

Probably not? But they should want to know every detail, Meg thought indignantly. They needed to know about the tapped phone and the way Mr. Lysikov was so friendly to everyone. For that matter, her father should show a little more interest. A lot was at stake. The interests of the country. And Irina's whole life.

Meg squashed the guilt again, and wandered into the kitchen where her mother sat at the table reading the morning paper. Falling into one of the kitchen chairs, Meg crossed her arms on the table and laid her head on her arms.

"Is it okay if Irina spends the night tonight?"

"Darling, I think that is a wonderful idea," Meg's mother said, putting down the paper. "I'm glad you two are friends. You make me so proud sometimes."

Meg smiled back. She was not absolutely sure that pride was warranted in this particular case, but her mother's comment pleased her anyway.

As she poured herself a bowl of bran flakes, Meg started reading the cereal boxes. Saturday was cold cereal day at the Donovans'. Meg's parents liked to sleep late, and Celia had the weekends off.

"Mom, is Celia poor?" Cold cereal reminded her of Celia's wonderful breakfasts, and that reminded her of what Irina had said — that Americans take advantage of Hispanics and that, in America, Celia could never be equal to the President.

Mrs. Donovan put down her paper. She looked mildly alarmed. "Well, she's not rich, but she's just bought a condominium. Why, did Celia say something?"

"No. I was just thinking," Meg said.

"You know, if Celia ever decided to leave, this family would fall apart." Mrs. Donovan looked out the window. Meg could see her comment had worried her mother.

"Mom, you make it sound like a divorce," Meg said. "Besides, Celia loves us. She would never leave."

"Of course, she loves us. But, if she got a better offer, she would have every right to take it. Are you helping her enough around the house?" Mrs. Donovan frowned at Meg.

"Sure, Mom. We set the table, and clean up our rooms, and empty the dishwasher, and put away the clean clothes. Dorie and I do everything practically."

Now that she really thought about it, though, she did sometimes slip when it came to doing her chores. Just yesterday, she had come home and all the clean clothes had already been carried upstairs and put in the drawers. That was Meg's job. She knew Celia would not say anything to her mother, but she resolved not to let it happen again. What if Celia left? What if somebody like Mrs. Bugayev came?

"Sorry, I forgot the laundry," Meg had said yesterday while Celia was waiting for her son to pick her up in his car. "Is something wrong with the buses?"

"No, *niña*, I'm just lazy," Celia had said, smiling. She stretched in the chair.

"Your back hurts," Meg had guessed. And she had been right on the mark. Celia had nodded and given her a hug.

"It stops hurting when I see him." Celia had moved to stand up, waving to her son, whose face had just appeared through one of the little windows in the front door.

Meg knew that Celia had come to the United States to work as a maid for a diplomatic family. She had finally become a permanent resident and sent for her son to join her. She didn't want him serving in the Salvadorean army while the war went on. He was now working as a mechanic. Celia said the job was *very* good. Meg figured that meant he made lots of money.

Meg's mother interrupted her thoughts. "You and Dorie need to help as much as you can. Celia's getting older, and the housework isn't getting easier."

"She's only fifty," Meg said in a matter-of-fact tone. She didn't want her mother to think she was arguing with her.

"She's been telling you kids that for years, honey." Meg's mother turned back to the paper.

If Meg had been a character in a cartoon, the drawing would have shown a ton of bricks falling on her. Meg had overlooked a fact, a fundamental piece of information about someone she thought she knew as well as her own mother. Incredible. Celia *had* been fifty for as long as Meg could remember.

"How old do you think she really is?" Meg asked, taking a bite of cereal.

"I have no idea. That's why we give her a present on the anniversary of the date she started with us. She won't tell me her birthday."

Was Celia too vain to tell her real birthday? Meg pictured her. She used no makeup, her hair was always worn up on her head in a bun, and she wore fresh-smelling and comfortable, but certainly not glamorous, dresses. Her dark-skinned face, pretty brown eyes, and gentle smile showed not one trace of vanity.

So if Celia wasn't vain, why wouldn't she give her age? Meg's own deduction surprised her. Was it possible Celia didn't know her birthday? Maybe there were no birth records kept in the village where she was born.

As she munched her cold cereal and stared out the kitchen window, Meg tried to imagine what it would be like not to know her own birthday. She wondered how many other things about Celia she didn't know. One thing about Celia she knew for sure. She didn't want Celia to leave — ever. Meg would lug the laundry up the stairs and back down again ten times a day if only it would keep Celia working at their house.

Suddenly David appeared, careening around the corner of the house on his bicycle, his legs stretched out on either side without touching the pedals. He stopped one inch short of the brick wall that surrounded the Donovans' back patio.

Meg's Saturday brightened. David always had good ideas about things to do. And he had remembered to park his bike in the backyard.

"Hi, Meg, Mrs. Donovan. What's for lunch?" David asked as he bounded in the kitchen door.

"Hi, David. Lunch? It's not noon for another half hour. Oh, well, why don't you kids order a pizza? I haven't been to the grocery store in a while. I'll treat." Mrs. Donovan smiled fondly at David. "Nice haircut," she added as she buried her face again in the newspaper.

"Mom, you are *great*," Meg said, pushing back her cereal bowl to save her appetite for pizza. There were times when her mother was absolutely perfect. Not only did they get pizza, but her mother had just won Meg a quarter bet.

After ordering the pizza and collecting her money, Meg told David about the hearing.

"Fantastic. I hope the FBI wants to interview me. I could be a witness at the guy's trial. I saw him, too, you know, at the gallery." David looked out the window at the house across the street. Then he turned quickly to face Meg. "Hey, I may be spending the night here tonight," he said in a conspiratorial tone. "My mom's going to call to see if it's all right. She and Dad have to go to Baltimore."

"That would be great. Irina may be coming, too. I invited her, but she hasn't told me yet whether she can come," Meg said. Just the memory of their secret walkie-talkie conversation the previous night brought a smile to her face. Her hand went to her pocket where she had put her ghostwriter developer pen just in case Irina sent her answer by secret message.

"That's the Russian girl? What's she like?"

"She's okay." Then Meg amended her endorsement. "But she's a government freak."

"A what?"

"You know. Some kids watch TV all the time

and they're television freaks. Some kids eat candy all the time and they're sweet freaks," Meg explained. "Well, she thinks about her government all the time and she likes to talk about it. She's a government freak."

"It sounds terminal. Is it contagious?"

The pizza arrived, and soon everybody in the house had followed its aroma into the kitchen. Ten minutes later, it was gone.

"C'mon, Meg." David did a romping slide step through the kitchen and out the back door.

"Where?" Meg called, striding quickly behind him.

"Just c'mon. Hurry!" David shouted. He was already on his bike and halfway down the side walkway to the front of the house.

Meg had to run to her bike and unlock it before she could follow him. He was already up the street when she finally got to the front of the house. She did a running jump onto her bike, grumbling to herself and wondering whether she should even try to catch him.

Then she saw what he was following. It was a large, black limousine. David must have seen it from the Donovans' window.

Meg managed to keep David in sight, but the limousine disappeared around a traffic circle. Finally, Meg had to stop completely. A red light and bumper-to-bumper traffic blocked her way. She saw David riding furiously on the sidewalk following several blocks behind the limousine, and then both disappeared around a curve in the road.

"Oh, brother," Meg muttered to herself. "Only David would think of chasing the Russians on bikes."

The light changed, and Meg pedaled furiously down the street in the direction she had last seen David.

"Hey, Meg, over here." David waved his arms from where he was stopped on the sidewalk as Meg flew by on the street. Then, lounging back in his bicycle seat with his arms crossed, he said, "What took you so long?" as Meg pulled up beside him.

"Not cute, David." Meg, flushed, sweaty, and exhausted, felt as though her feet were absorbing all the heat from the sidewalk and her face was radiating it back into the atmosphere.

David nodded toward the high, beige brick wall on the far side of the street. Black wrought-iron gates closed over the entrance.

"They went in there," he said. "Before we got here, I caught up to them at a stop sign and Irina waved to me. How did she know me? We've never really met."

"She's probably seen you hanging around my house," Meg said, still breathless. Everybody else in the world probably sees you hanging around my house, she thought, why not Irina?

"I saw them getting in the car from your house. There was the driver, Irina, that spy, and a woman who looked like a large troll."

Meg leaned her bicycle against a tree and fell down in the grass laughing aloud. "A TROLL. I knew she reminded me of something."

David grinned and sat down Indian-style next to her.

"This place looks like jail," he said.

"It must be the compound. That's where a lot of Soviet diplomats live," Meg answered, raising herself up on her elbows to look at the wall.

"Are they trying to keep people out or in?"

"Both, maybe. That troll tries to keep Irina in and me out of their house," Meg answered. "It seems to be a Russian kind of thing." She lay back down. She was starting to feel dreamy, resting in the shade after that long bike ride.

"Y'know, Meg, I've been thinking." David absentmindedly started picking at the grass beside him.

"Uh-oh." Meg closed her eyes.

"Y'know, that boyfriend-girlfriend thing we talked about on the phone?" David began.

"Mmmm." Meg knew she should be alert for this conversation but her muscles felt too weak to sit up, and the sun was too bright to keep her eyes open while lying down.

"Well, I was thinking that since I need a girlfriend, just for convenience, y'know, I might as well have you for a girlfriend. You're the only girl who's really any fun to be with and, if the girls at my school knew I had a girlfriend at another school, they might leave me alone."

Meg sat up and opened her eyes.

"So, what am I going to do for a boyfriend?"

"I'll be your boyfriend," David said evenly.

"You're too short," Meg countered.

"I'm growing. My dad is 5′10″, and I'll be as tall as he is or even taller."

"Yeah, but now you're short." Meg wished she were anywhere but having this conversation with David. "It just won't work."

"Nothing has to work. It wouldn't be real. We'll just stay like we are now. And then if we get real girlfriends or boyfriends, we'll just tell each other." David had not been convinced by Meg's protests. In fact, he had hardly listened to them.

"I don't know." Meg shook her head.

"Well, it doesn't matter. We don't have to decide until school starts again. That's when that girl I said would be my girlfriend gets back." David sighed. "I've gotta think of something else before then."

Lucky girl, Meg thought. David wanted her for a girlfriend because she was out of town. When she gets back, he'll drop her. He doesn't know *anything* about love and romance. He'd probably fall asleep watching *Gone With the Wind*.

David changed the subject. "You know, the way

112

Irina was waving to me, I almost thought she wanted to tell me something. She threw a scrap of paper out of the window. I thought it might be a note but it's blank," David said.

"Paper? What paper?" Meg said abruptly. "Where is it?"

"Right here." David pulled a crumpled piece of paper from his jeans pocket.

Meg tugged her ghostwriter developer pen from her pocket and tore off the cap. As David watched over her shoulder, Meg scribbled over the paper. The message appeared immediately.

Dear Meg,

Mrs. Bugayev found me with your walkie-talkie and took it away. Now we have to go to the embassy to make a report on your family. Mrs. Bugayev says I should never see you again, but Papa is on our side. I hope that your family can be cleared by the security division. Then we can have a sleeping party.

Your friend,
Irina

"Cleared? What does that mean?" David looked puzzled.

"I'm not sure. Maybe they want to make sure we're not criminals or terrorists," Meg replied.

"Or maybe that we don't have anything contagious like head lice or pinworms."

Until now, Meg had been unsure about Irina spending the night. She didn't want to give Irina endless opportunities to turn missionary. But now that Mrs. Bugayev had taken a stand and was trying to turn the entire Soviet embassy against the Donovans, it had become a question of honor. Irina *had* to come over. If Irina were not granted permission to come to the "sleeping party," Meg decided, she and David would plan a jailbreak.

12

No jailbreak was necessary. That evening, Irina arrived just a little after David did. She was wearing her American clothes. The Harvard sweatshirt was smaller than it had been before. It still hung loosely around her body, but the sleeves were two inches above Irina's wrists.

Meg easily deduced that Mrs. Bugayev had run Irina's sweatshirt through the hot cycle of the dryer.

"Hi. I understand you're a fan of Karl Marx," David said, grinning.

"Why, yes. Of course," Irina responded, looking down at her feet.

Meg waited for Irina to launch into her monologue about Soviet equality. It didn't happen. She was probably waiting for the right moment to convert him.

David stood, his head cocked to one side and his hands on his hips. Meg noticed that he and Irina were about the same height.

"Well, I sort of like economics, too. I'm in line

for the paper route in our neighborhood. I get it this fall when the guy who has it now goes away to school. I'll probably be pretty rich by Christmas," David said.

C'mon, Irina, Meg thought. Paperboys are an exploited underclass, aren't they? But Irina once again said nothing.

"Hey, kids, how about a movie?" Mr. Donovan loped down the stairs into the entrance hall. He took the steps two at a time.

"There's a double feature Superman playing," David said enthusiastically. "I've seen 'em both. They're great."

Mr. Donovan laughed. "Sounds good to me. I haven't seen a Superman movie for years. How 'bout you girls?" He nodded toward Meg.

Meg hesitated. "Uh, I dunno, Dad." Saturday night was date night. What if she saw some of her friends at the theater and what if they had dates?

"It sounds splendid," Irina spoke up, grinning.

Meg was tempted. She'd seen the first but not the second movie. She *did* like Superman, and her dad would be paying. She calculated the risks. The theater would be dark. She could always slouch in her seat if she saw somebody from school. She could carry her raincoat with the hood, as an added precaution. She decided to go.

As they emerged from the movie, Irina was deep in conversation with David. "It shows how change is needed," Irina was saying. "The forces of good must rise up to battle injustice. Superman represents truth and loyalty and goodness, and he always wins, doesn't he?"

Meg tried to catch David's eye and give him an "I told you so" grin, but he was looking at Irina.

"Yeah," he said, agreeing with a heartfelt sigh. "Superman's great."

Mr. Donovan led the group toward the ice-cream parlor next to the theater. He pulled open the door, and Meg started to walk in. She stopped mid-step and shrunk back.

There was Lacey Darcy and six other kids from school. They had taken up a long table at the far end of the room, but Meg could hear them laughing and shouting from the front entrance. That was one thing Meg did not want on a Saturday night — a sympathetic look from Lacey Darcy.

"Uh, Dad, just a second. I gotta put on my raincoat," Meg stammered, backing out the door.

Mr. Donovan, still holding the door open, frowned at Meg.

"Meg, it's not raining. What is the matter with you, girl? Are you getting sick?" Mr. Donovan did not sound worried. He sounded impatient.

Meg could not move. Her feet were stuck to the sidewalk.

David, waiting to go in, looked through the window and saw Meg's friends. "Hey, Mr. Donovan. Why don't we get a couple of gallons and take them home? Maybe Mrs. Donovan and Dorie would like some." David spoke in his most polite tone.

"Good idea, David. I'll get it. You sure you're okay, Meg?"

Meg nodded. Mr. Donovan walked inside and stood at the counter.

While Irina pattered on about *The Daily Planet* representing the voice of the people, and Lois Lane, the innocence of the victims of exploitation, David gave Meg a thumbs-up.

Gratitude flowed through Meg with such force it made her feel weak. What she needed to parade in front of her schoolmates was a tall, dark, and handsome date. Walking in with David, Irina, and her father would make her feel more than ever like the Human Library. She returned David's thumbs-up with a heartfelt sigh of relief.

At home, after ice cream, Meg followed David down to the basement playroom. Irina stayed at the kitchen table, talking quietly with Mrs. Donovan. "Thanks, David. Back at the ice-cream parlor, you know," Meg said softly, so no one in the kitchen could hear.

"Yeah. I saw those friends of yours and figured you wouldn't want them to see you with your dad," David said as he laid his bright red sleeping bag on the carpet in front of the TV. "They could see I was with Irina, and you didn't have a date."

Sudden anger welled up in Meg. David and Irina

had *not* been on a date. She swallowed her outrage. After all, she had come down to thank David for helping her. She did not want to lose her temper with him just because he rewrote a little history. "Good-night, David." Meg turned to go upstairs.

"Hey, just a second, I want to ask you something. Do you think I could ask Irina to be my girlfriend? She'd be perfect. Her dad would never let her go out with me, and I wouldn't have to spend any money on her." David stopped arranging his sleeping bag, sat back on his heels, and looked up at her.

"That is really sick, David." This time Meg did not try to hide her feelings. Just that afternoon, David had asked *her* to be his girlfriend. He hadn't even waited for a definitive "no." He was already trying to figure out whether Irina would be an even better no-fuss, no-expense girlfriend. Didn't he think girls had feelings?

David looked shocked. "Aw, c'mon, Meg. Not sick. Smart." He recovered quickly and grinned. "You know what's really sick, *sick*? Slinking around on Saturday night, hiding from those great buddies of yours."

It was Meg's turn to be surprised. Hiding from her friends? Was that what David thought she was doing?

She looked at his grinning face and did what came naturally. She crossed her eyes, stuck her thumbs in her ears, wriggled her fingers, shook her head, and leaned forward from the waist. It was one of the best full-body Bronx cheers she had ever done.

"I take it back. I take it back," David said, cringing. "You better stay in hiding another couple of years."

Without saying another word, Meg walked with as much dignity as she could muster up the stairs, her chin in the air.

" 'Night, Meg," David called behind her.

The Bronx cheer made her feel a little better, but it was only a temporary lift. All in all, for Meg it had been a humiliating evening. She'd stood there outside the ice-cream parlor as though she were a creature from social Siberia. Then David had treated her as if she were expendable.

If only her best friend Kathy were spending the night instead of David and Irina, Meg thought. Kathy would help her figure things out, turn it all into a funny joke, make her laugh about it. In fact, if Kathy were in town, the two of them would probably have been included in the group of kids at the ice-cream parlor. Hanging around with a Russian government freak and a short boy with a cardboard heart suddenly made Meg feel more lonely than if she had spent Saturday night home alone.

By the time Meg walked into her bedroom, Irina

was already in a long nightgown. Her hair fell loosely over one shoulder, and she brushed it as she sat on the bottom bunk staring out the window at her house across the street.

Her hair is beautiful, Meg thought grudgingly. Meg always had wanted long hair but when she let hers grow, being so curly, it only got thicker, never longer. She was glad Irina looked so pretty. It made it easier to be mad at her, which was exactly what she wanted to be.

"My father is working late again, I guess. The car's not there. Mrs. Bugayev must be in bed already," Irina mused.

"Mmmmmmm," Meg responded. How could I have ever thought she could take the place of Kathy, even temporarily? She's nothing like Kathy.

"He is working on something very, very important," Irina continued proudly.

Like spying, Meg thought. And pretty soon, he's going to be picked up by the FBI.

"Do you like Celia?" Irina asked abruptly.

"Of course," Meg answered brusquely, struggling with the quick change of topic.

"I don't think Mrs. Bugayev likes me," Irina said in a matter-of-fact tone. She stopped brushing her hair, placed her brush carefully in her purse, and climbed into bed.

"How come?" Meg asked, still standing, arms

crossed, in the middle of the room. She didn't feel much like talking, but her curiosity got the better of her.

"I know she's worried about my safety, but she doesn't want me to do anything. Remember we went to the embassy today to get a special clearance just so I could come tonight? She has not said anything to me since. But she's been slamming drawers and things. Tonight at dinner, she gave me the smallest piece of cake and it was all crumbs. I think she might have smashed it on purpose. I know she's going to be mad at me for a long time."

"Yeah. Well, she's gotta give back my walkie-talkie," Meg said unsympathetically. Irina didn't answer.

"Your dad ought to fire her," Meg muttered and grabbed her pajamas from the hook in her closet, turned off the light, and climbed to the top bunk to change and crawl under the covers.

"She was assigned to us in Moscow," Irina said quietly.

"You know what, Irina? I think it's really dumb for a government to make people who don't like each other live together." There. Meg had finally said something mean about the Soviet Union, and it really felt good. She pulled the sheets up to her chin. She spoke again into the darkness. "Your country is not so perfect, you know." There again.

Meg waited for Irina's response. She wanted to

fight with her — have it out with her once and for all. Irina deserved it. Acting as though her country were heaven on earth. It was disgusting. If it had been Kathy in that lower bunk instead of Irina, they would have spent the evening laughing at one another's oatmeal facials and making homemade pizza. *That* would have been a fun Saturday night. And now, to add to her list of grievances against Irina, David wanted Irina to be his girlfriend. That was the worst part of all.

Meg did not expect Irina's reaction. At first, there was no reaction. There was no sound or movement in the bed below Meg. Five minutes passed. Then Meg heard a sniffle.

Meg had made Irina cry. Strong-willed Irina, crying. In a matter of minutes, she'd been transformed into the shy, scared Irina at the carnival. And it was Meg's fault. A secret message suddenly flashed through Meg's mind. "I want to be your friend." Irina, who had defied Mrs. Bugayev and would never be taken in by Lacey Darcy, was crying. And then Meg remembered Irina's gold pin. It was now the crown jewel in her badge collection, just over there on the dresser.

Meg suddenly wanted the bold Irina back.

"It doesn't matter, Irina." She said the first thing that came into her head.

"It does, though, you see. I am supposed to be like an ambassador, telling Americans the good news about my country. They told me so in a class

I took just before I came here," Irina said. She spoke in a low tone, as though willing self-control. "I've so wanted to be like my mother, strong and good and teaching people things. I guess I have been — how do you say it — painful."

"No — a pain. Listen, Irina, it doesn't matter," Meg said again quickly. "And about Mrs. Bugayev. You ought to tell your dad. He'd help."

"He's too busy." Now Irina's voice sounded muffled, as though it came from inside her pillow.

"Parents are always busy. You just have to interrupt them. They like to be told stuff. It makes them feel like they're good parents." Meg talked fast. She didn't want to listen to silence again. "I remember when I was just a kid my parents took a course on how to raise children. There was a whole chapter in their book about helping to solve kids' problems. I used to make up problems just so they could help me. It made them feel really good. Until they figured out what I was doing. Then they made me stop."

"But my father has been so sad since my mother died. I can't make him sadder." Irina's voice sounded shaky, but it was no longer coming from inside her pillow.

There was that silence again. A new thought tumbled into Meg's head. There was only one Irina, not two, a girl who loved her mother and her country. But then she'd lost her mother and had to move away from her country. Meg quickly broke the silence again.

"Well, let's just get rid of Mrs. Bugayev. It's her you don't like, right?"

"I can't get in trouble," Irina said, hesitating. Meg thought Irina might already be thinking about a new life without Mrs. Bugayev. A minute later, Irina asked, "How would we do it?"

"I don't know. We'd have to have a plan. Let's ask David. He always has good ideas." She threw back the blanket and slid down to the floor.

"Right now?" Irina asked.

"Yeah. Here, catch." Meg threw Irina her pink satin robe with the white ruffle around the neck, and put on her old white terrycloth one. Meg wanted to be especially kind to Irina, not just out of guilt — although there *was* some of that — but also because when Irina was sad and scared, it made Meg sad, too. That's what friendship's like, she thought for a fleeting moment. Then she saw how lovely Irina looked in her best robe, and wondered if she'd overdone it. Too late now.

The two girls tiptoed through the quiet house. The moon shone through the window at the top of the stairs, making shadows of tree branches dance all the way down the staircase. When they got down to the basement playroom, they found David watching a Godzilla movie, the television lighting the entire room.

13

"**H**aunt her," David suggested. "We'll clang things in the middle of the night and pour ketchup on clothes in the dryer. She'll think it's blood." David had turned the TV volume down but still stole looks at the screen.

"I don't think Mrs. Bugayev is afraid of ghosts," Irina said.

"How about just disobeying her all the time, sassing back and stuff? You could be so bad that she can't stand her job and quits," Meg suggested.

"Oh, I couldn't do that," Irina said, looking frightened. Her hands were clutched together in her lap as she sat on her knees on the carpet.

"Well, we could have a telegram sent in Russian asking her to come home. Does she have a sister or somebody who could get sick?" Meg asked.

"No. Well, yes. She does have a sister, but then she would get to Moscow and find out the trick. She would know it was me somehow. No. We can't do that. Maybe we'd better not try to get rid of

Mrs. Bugayev," Irina said sadly. "I don't think anything will work."

"Hey, Irina, don't worry. Meg and I will think of something, won't we, Meg?" David sounded confident.

But, as it turned out, it was Irina who thought of something. The next morning at breakfast, Irina ate only two bites of the pancakes Mr. Donovan made while David, Meg, and Dorie asked for one after another. Finally, Meg noticed that Irina was signaling her and David to go upstairs.

Up in Meg's room, Irina closed the door behind them.

"Hey, it's me. Can I come in?" Dorie knocked hard on the door just as the three were settling onto the floor.

Meg looked at the others. No one objected.

"Okay. Come in," Meg shouted. "But no talking, Dorie. You can just listen," Meg said more quietly as Dorie closed the door behind her. "We're thinking of a plan to get rid of Irina's housekeeper."

"Murder?" Dorie whispered the word, her eyes wide.

"No, my dearest and darling little sister, not murder. Now, hush."

Dorie flopped onto the bed. She put her chin in her hands and listened, squinting. Meg knew it was her look of deepest concentration.

"Mrs. Bugayev is writing a report to the embassy. I overheard her mention it to my father,"

Irina began in a hushed tone. "It might be possible for us to find it."

"Yeah, what do we do with it?" David asked expectantly. It was clear he was already sold on the idea, no matter what it was.

"You gave me the idea when you said let's have a letter sent from her sister." Irina nodded toward Meg. "That wouldn't work, but this might."

Irina leaned forward to make the circle smaller. Dorie stretched so far over the edge of the bed, she almost fell off.

"At the end of the report, we would add a sentence suggesting that she might like to serve the motherland in a more challenging position. She would ask, most politely, for another job. We would have to write it just right, so it would seem to come from her," Irina said.

"In Russian," Meg added, nodding. "So they would send her somewhere else, give her another job, because of that?"

"They might. And if they did, she could not question it. She has to take whatever job she is assigned," Irina said authoritatively. "It might not work, but, if it did . . ." her voice trailed off, a smile of relief on her face.

"It's a great plan," Meg said enthusiastically. "We'll do whatever it takes."

"Good thinking, Irina," David added.

"How do we do it?" Dorie asked.

The four looked at each other blankly, as though

soaking the plan in and, for the first time, sensing danger.

David spoke first. "Okay. We gotta get this report. The question is when," he said in his take-charge voice.

"This afternoon, an embassy limousine will take Mrs. Bugayev to the grocery store," Irina said. "I will not go. I'll tell her I'm not feeling well and want to sleep."

"What about your dad?" Meg asked.

"He'll probably be working. If not, we'll have to do it some other time."

"So it's this afternoon," David announced.

Irina flushed. Meg thought she was going to back down or at least postpone the attempt.

"Yes. We must do it today," Irina said firmly.

"Can I come?" Dorie asked.

"It's too dangerous, Dorie. If Mrs. Bugayev comes home, we don't know what she might do," Meg said in a stern voice.

"Meg," Dorie whined, "I'm your junior partner."

"Oh, she can come," David interrupted. "She can be our lookout."

"When Mrs. Bugayev has gone to the store and it is safe, I will send you a secret signal," Irina whispered.

"Open the front curtains. We couldn't miss that," Meg said.

"Okay. That's it," David said. He put out his

hand, palm down. Meg covered it with hers. And Irina put her hand gently on Meg's. Just as they squeezed hands and wished each other good luck, Dorie bounced off the bed and added her hand to the top.

Reverently, she whispered, "This is just like Nancy Drew!"

14

"Why are you three kids hopping around the dining room on such a gorgeous day?" Meg's mother called from the kitchen. "Go spend that energy outside."

At the dining room table, David was huddled over a Scrabble board game with only three words on it. His foot was banging rhythmically against the leg of the table. Meg had just laid down a word and jumped up to look out the window. Dorie was skipping around the table, her pigtails flying. Mrs. Donovan did not see the three of them freeze in place when she spoke.

"Okay, Mom. We'll go out right away," Meg replied.

David hurried out the front door, followed by Dorie tiptoeing behind him. Meg sauntered casually out the door and closed it behind her. She caught a glimpse of her mother shaking her head in bewilderment.

"Dorie, you almost blew it. How come you tiptoed?" Meg whispered, frowning at her sister. Meg hoped her mother was not suspicious.

"Sorry," Dorie said, avoiding Meg's eyes.

Meg sat down next to David on the front stoop. Dorie began to kick small sticks and leaves around the yard, her hands behind her back.

"That woman has been gone for ten minutes. How come Irina hasn't given us the signal?" David asked, staring at the house across the street.

"Maybe she's lost her courage," Meg said. The more Meg thought about it, the more she thought Irina might do just that. What if Mrs. Bugayev caught them? Irina would be guilty of breaking and entering, forgery, and attempting to deceive the authorities — serious offenses in any of Meg's favorite books. Meg thought that the authorities in Moscow, whoever they were, might put somebody in jail for that, maybe for life. Starting at eleven years old, it would be decades before Irina would even have gray hair, much less be dead. Could the Soviet government do anything to American kids? Meg wondered if she were losing her own courage.

"Maybe that mean housekeeper locked her in her room," Dorie whispered loudly as she kicked a stone up onto the sidewalk near Meg and David.

"Nope. There it is." David pointed excitedly at the house across the street.

Meg jumped up and Dorie clapped. The curtains were opening slowly, but steadily. The house took on the look of a four-eyed monster, one eye open, staring at them across the street.

It is three o'clock in the afternoon, Meg reminded herself. This is broad daylight. That is not a monster across the street. It is just a house. Meg remembered her Sherlock Holmes lineage and took a deep breath. It actually did steady her nerves.

"Now, everybody act natural," David said. "Dorie, you keep kicking that rock across the street. We'll just walk on over." He started down the sidewalk, whistling "Yankee Doodle."

"Just a second," Meg said. She opened the front door. "M-o-o-o-m," she shouted. "We're going over to Irina's."

"That's nice, honey," her mother's voice came back.

Good, she's not suspicious, Meg thought to herself. Her mother's voice had sounded so normal, it made Meg almost smile at her own fears. But not quite.

As David and Meg climbed the front steps to Irina's house, Irina opened the door. She smiled weakly and motioned them inside.

They had to wait at the door for Dorie. She was trying to kick her rock over the curb. On the third try, it ricocheted against the curb and flew under a parked car. Dorie, still standing in the street, put her hands on her hips and looked up at the others.

Sometimes Meg could read Dorie's mind. She knew right now, for example, that Dorie had been surprised to learn that tiptoeing out the front door had been the wrong thing to do. She was trying to make up for her mistake by following David's instructions to kick the stone across the street.

"C'mon, Dorie. It doesn't matter," Meg shouted. Dorie's grin of relief filled her face and she scrambled up the steps.

The four started immediately up the stairs to the second floor. The house seemed less sinister with the sunlight coming in through the living room window. Less sinister, but more dusty. A thin film covered the table by the window and particles danced in the light.

David sneezed. "Doesn't she ever vacuum?" he whispered.

"Sometimes," Irina replied distractedly. She had a key, a pen, and a sheet of blank paper clutched in one hand. She seemed to be concentrating on her feet as she marched up the stairs.

Meg's stomach felt funny, and strength seemed to be seeping out of her legs. She wondered if she would have to sit down and rest halfway up. Irina sure has guts, Meg thought. She made it up the stairs without stopping by sliding her feet into the marks in the dust left by Irina's shoes.

"It took me awhile to find the key. It was in a different vase," Irina mumbled as she turned at the top of the stairs and stood before a closed door.

She slipped the key into the lock and turned it. She looked up at Meg.

"We're with you, Irina," Meg whispered. She didn't know what Irina had wanted her to say, but that seemed to reassure Irina because she turned the doorknob, opened the door, and walked into the dark room.

"Hey, somebody turn on the lights," Dorie said as she followed the others in.

Irina flipped the lightswitch and an overhead light came on. More than electric lights are needed to brighten this room, Meg thought. Dark wooden shutters covered the windows, a single bed was covered with a gray, woolen banket, and a small desk with papers spread over it stood in a corner. A man with sharp, deepset eyes and a mustache and goatee peered at them from the only picture decorating the walls.

"Is that her husband?" Meg whispered, looking at the picture.

"No. Lenin," Irina replied aloud. She was already at the desk, going through the papers, carefully picking them up at the corners, squinting at them, and replacing them on the desk.

"It stinks in here," Dorie complained.

"Desenex," Meg said, recognizing the odor. "She has athlete's foot."

"And licorice. I smell licorice," David added. "I wonder where she keeps it."

"Here it is. The report," Irina said quietly. She

let out a deep breath. "Her handwriting is so small. I'm going to have to practice it." She sat down at the desk, laid the blank piece of paper on top of the report, and began to trace, slowly and carefully, her nose almost touching the paper. David and Meg leaned over her, careful not to block the light.

Suddenly, Irina stopped. She pulled the report out from under her own paper and stared at it with her mouth open.

"You found a good place to add a sentence?" Meg asked. She didn't want to hurry Irina, but the desire to get out of this room and this house was becoming urgent.

"This is so strange." Irina ignored Meg's question. "Here she is saying what was in my father's suitcoat pocket. She even names the restaurant on a matchbook cover."

"And here she writes the amount of money my father spent for my American clothes," Irina said, pointing to a sentence, even though Meg and David could not read the strange Russian handwriting. "I knew she didn't like him doing that," she added.

Meg and David exchanged glances. It was hard to imagine Celia caring what Meg's parents bought for her, as long as the clothes could be washed in the machine.

Irina flinched and caught her breath.

"What is it? What did she say?" Meg, too, stared at the report. It told her nothing.

"It's my secret diary." Irina threw the report down on the desk and covered it with her hand. "She has copied here my entry from yesterday." Tears rose in Irina's eyes as she covered her mouth with her other hand.

"She's not nice," Dorie said breathlessly.

"She's a witch," Meg said under her breath.

"She's a spy," David said.

The three gathered around Irina, who was beginning to sob quietly. Dorie threw her arms around Irina's neck. Meg wanted to comfort her, too, but Dorie was already there, so she handed Irina a crumpled tissue from her pocket. David put his hand on the back of her chair and then slipped it forward to rest gently on Irina's shoulder.

They all heard the noise downstairs at the same time. The front door slammed. The entranceway floorboards creaked. There were footsteps on the stairs. Someone was coming!

Meg looked frantically around the room. They couldn't all fit in the closet.

"Yikes!" Dorie whispered and headed for the bed. She threw the gray wool blanket over her body and scrunched up into a ball.

"We forgot the lookout," David groaned softly. He shrugged his shoulders helplessly, looking at the lump Dorie made on the bed.

No lookout, Meg scolded herself silently. We didn't even close the door. Whoever it is can't miss us.

Meg's heartbeat filled the room.

Irina dried her eyes with the tissue, straightened in her chair, and turned to face the doorway.

15

"**M**y Irina! Where are you? We will go to the zoo," a deep voice boomed through the house. A second later, Mr. Lysikov filled the door-frame.

Meg blew air out quietly between her teeth.

The pleasant look on Mr. Lysikov's face changed. His eyes traveled from Meg to David and landed on Irina with a thud. His bushy eye-brows formed a straight, dark line above his eyes.

His voice was low and controlled when he addressed his daughter.

Meg knew exactly what he said, even though it was in Russian: What in the world were they doing in Mrs. Bugayev's room?

Irina raised her chin and said just a few words. Mr. Lysikov barked back and, in two steps, was towering above her, his posture stiff and his hands clenched behind his back.

"Irina," Meg said urgently. "You've got to tell him everything." Her voice shook.

Irina and her father turned to look at Meg as though they had forgotten she was there. Neither of them spoke to her. Mr. Lysikov turned back to his daughter.

Irina started talking slowly in Russian, though she was still looking at Meg. Her hands lay limply in her lap.

As Irina talked, Meg could tell that Mr. Lysikov's anger was leaving him. He unclenched his hands and, still listening intently, backed slowly toward the bed and sat down.

"Help." A muffled cry came from the bed.

Mr. Lysikov jumped up in surprise and pulled the blanket off the bed in one swoosh. There was Dorie curled up with her eyes squeezed shut.

"Another one," Mr. Lysikov mumbled in English. He recovered his composure quickly. "Are you all right, my dear?" he asked, leaning down to look into Dorie's face.

Dorie opened her eyes wide. "Yeah, I just didn't want you to sit on me," she said, pulling herself up.

Mr. Lysikov patted Dorie on the back, sat back down on the bed, and turned again to Irina. He asked her what seemed to Meg to be a very long question.

Irina picked up Mrs. Bugayev's report and held it on her lap. She spoke softly but clearly, looking down at the paper.

Mr. Lysikov held out his hand. Irina brought

the report to her father, and he pulled her onto his knee while he read it. Irina interrupted his reading to point to a passage and tears welled in her eyes again.

That's the part about her diary, Meg thought. Good, she's telling him everything. And he's listening so carefully. It reminded her of that course on raising kids that her parents had taken when she was little. Maybe parents in the Soviet Union take the same course. She decided then and there that she liked Mr. Lysikov and didn't care if he was a spy.

But then she remembered that others cared a lot. Invisible people from the FBI were right now preparing the case against him. They were using Meg's evidence. It made her feel suddenly ill. "We gotta go, you guys," she said quietly.

David stood up quickly and Dorie hopped off the bed.

"Thank you for helping Irina," Mr. Lysikov said.

Irina laid her head on her father's shoulder.

They trailed out, Dorie last, chattering, "Oh, that's okay. We liked it. It was kind of an adventure. Meg thought there was a spy here. So she got to be friends with Irina — you know, to scout the place out. But now we know who the bad guy is, or I mean the bad lady, so I guess the adventure's over. Oh, well, we can be just regular friends now. Bye."

Meg and David froze on the stairs. Meg's hand went to her mouth in shock. David grimaced and motioned with a wild wave of his arm for Dorie to hurry up. The three clambered down the stairs, out the front door, and across the street.

The next few days were torture for Meg, mainly because very little happened. It was as though a dramatic video had stuck on hold. As much as she wanted to see the rest of the movie, she had a sinking suspicion it might have an unhappy ending. Why didn't Mr. Lysikov escape, now that he knew his cover was blown?

Every day, sometimes several times a day, Meg checked the planter for messages. Nothing. In fact, the geraniums were dying. Their leaves were going yellow, and the blossoms were turning black. So much attention, so little care. Meg wondered if she'd been as careless with Irina as she'd been with the geraniums. She never had really tried to understand her.

One notable development occurred at the Lysikovs'. A new woman appeared. She wore her hair short and fluffy and, even from across the street, her face looked kind. Meg refused to make a deduction about whether she was Irina's aunt, her new stepmother, Mary Poppins, a robot. Meg didn't care. Somehow the fun had gone out of detective work.

And, then, one morning at breakfast, exactly four long days after the scene in Mrs. Bugayev's bedroom, Meg's dad let out a whoop from behind the newspaper. He turned it around and jabbed his finger at a headline. "Hey, look at this. So that's what Lysikov's been working on!"

Meg's mother read it aloud: " 'U.S., SOVIETS AGREE ON JOINT MEASURES AGAINST TERRORISM. CIA and KGB to Share Intelligence.' That's very good news," she said enthusiastically.

"You knew about this, Dad." Meg's heart, sitting in the basement for days, sank to the center of the earth.

"Well, yes, though not exactly. The FBI told me that the meeting you saw at the East Building between the aide to the Secretary of State and Mr. Lysikov was authorized, so I figured something like this was being worked out." Mr. Donovan leaned back in his chair. "They weren't pleased an eleven-year-old had uncovered the connection."

Meg kept staring at her father. An eleven-year-old who, despite being a direct descendent of the most famous detective in the world, had bungled the biggest case she'd ever handled.

"I couldn't tell you, honey," he continued apologetically, looking kindly at Meg. "Even the fact that the meeting was authorized was highly classified. Only about six people in our government knew about it."

"So that means Irina's father *is* a good guy?"

Dorie was delighted. "I knew he was a good guy all the time!"

Meg dragged herself up from the breakfast table and headed for the overstuffed chair in the living room. Where had she gone wrong? I made an honest mistake, she tried to tell herself — solid facts, weak analysis. Everybody in the business makes a mistake at one time or another.

But, try as she might, dark, heavy thoughts seeped through. She'd made a BIG mistake. She'd abused a friendship, used it to get something that would bring glory to herself and disaster to her friend. And now she had nothing, neither glory nor her friend.

Suddenly she saw it from Irina's point of view. Meg had been worse than disloyal. She had betrayed Irina's friendship.

Dorie ambled lazily into the room and plopped down on the armrest of the overstuffed chair, draping her arm across the back. "Whatsa matter, Meg? Isn't it good Mr. Lysikov's not a spy?"

Meg dismissed the idea of blaming everything on Dorie and her big mouth. No sense adding self-deception to her newly realized list of character flaws. "I guess so, Dorie, but, you know, I've really screwed up."

"You mean we. I'm your junior partner. What'd we do?" Dorie frowned, trying to puzzle it out.

Under ordinary circumstances, Meg would have laughed aloud. Good old Dorie. Taking that junior partner stuff so seriously, wanting half of everything, even if it was the blame.

As it was, Meg managed a weak smile. "Well, I — I mean we — were after Mr. Lysikov because I — I mean we — thought he was a spy. But I — we — were wrong, and now Irina probably hates us." Now that she'd said it out loud, the situation seemed even worse. Sudden tears welled in her eyes.

Dorie's stopped frowning. "Oh, that. It's all right, partner. Ya just gotta write her another secret note. Say we're sorry. She likes you a lot."

Meg sniffed and stared at Dorie through blurry eyes. Could Dorie be right? It might work. Meg wanted Irina's friendship back. Of course, Irina had never been like Kathy. Meg knew that now. But courageous and serious and thoughtful Irina was unique among Meg's friends, and not only because she came from thousands of miles away. A secret apology was definitely worth a try.

"Thanks, Dorie," Meg said, thinking already about what she would say. "I will."

16

Dear Irina,

I know you cannot forgive me and you must not. I've been horrid. I'm returning your gold pin, but I will remember you always and will forever be sorry.

Meg

The phone rang half an hour after her secret message, wrapped around the gold pin, was delivered.

"It's Irina. Can you come over?"

When Irina opened the door, they looked at each other shyly. Meg, for one of the few times in her life, had nothing to say, so when Irina hugged her and went through the funny cheek-rubbing ritual, Meg didn't mind at all.

"We cannot go to my room. I am putting up pretty wallpaper. Our new housekeeper, she is so wonderful, knows how to do it and she's helping me."

Meg followed Irina to the patio. "What's happened to Mrs. Bugayev?"

"She's gone. I'll tell you about her." Irina sat down and motioned to Meg to sit beside her. She spoke in a hushed tone. "Mrs. Bugayev was really a spy! And we caught her!" Irina looked around, leaned even closer to Meg, her eyes widening. "There are some in the KGB who do not want *glasnost*. They do not want to cooperate with the United States. She was working for them, gathering information about my father that they could use to try to discredit him. They thought they could wreck what he was trying to do. Instead, my father embarrassed them by exposing what they were doing. We did a very good thing — we helped my father and my country and your country." It was the best political speech Irina had ever made.

To Meg, the information was like cool water on a sunburn. It fell over her, soothing and calming her. It almost made her forget the suffering of the last few days. But not quite. She wanted to make total amends.

"Irina, I'm sorry. About everything. At first, I did want to pretend to be friends because of your father. I thought I might catch him spying or something. It seems so silly, really, now. But,

147

then, it got to be different. I really liked you all by yourself."

Irina lifted her eyebrows and pursed her lips. Even now, Meg could tell the memory of Dorie's words was painful.

"I was angry with you at first. But I have to tell you something, too. There is much we still have to learn about each other." Irina opened her fist to reveal the gold pin lying on the palm of her hand. She held it steadily in front of her.

"My father tells me now that this is not gold. I think I knew that but I told you the opposite because I know how much Americans like gold and I wanted you to like me." Irina's eyes were glued to the pin in her hand.

Meg knew a confession when she heard one. Relief that she'd been forgiven filled her, and her first thought was to help Irina over the embarrassing moment.

"Well, *my* father saw me wearing it and he said it's very valuable because the United States didn't go to the Moscow Olympics and nobody here has one. So it's just as good as gold, really."

Irina smiled gratefully at Meg, and Meg grinned back.

Later that day, Meg and David were sitting on the front stoop of Meg's house. They were waiting for an inspired idea for the afternoon. David slumped against the house, and Meg fingered the pin glittering on her light blue T-shirt.

She could still feel the glow from her conversation with Irina that morning. She'd *felt* a spy in that house, and there'd *been* a spy in that house. Her instincts were reliable; she just needed a little more experience in analysis. She'd work on it. No problem.

Meg sighed dreamily. She couldn't wait to tell her junior partner, who was now at the pool. It had been a great case. And serious stuff, too. Much more important than Mrs. McGillicutty's missing brooch. She and Irina and David and Dorie had probably brought about world peace.

Then suddenly, like summer lightning on a dark night, a thought came to her. It made so many things clear. Irina was direct, resourceful, and brave — so brave there was a very good chance she had Sherlock Holmes blood in her veins, too. That would mean they were cousins.

"Do 'ya think Irina has any more of those pins?" David asked.

"Mmmmm. Maybe." Meg pulled herself reluctantly out of her reverie. "She has an incredible button and badge collection. Things that look official, like they might've belonged to an emperor."

"I might just take my collection over and see if there's anything she wants to trade." David squinted.

"You really like her, too, don't you?" She thought it and asked it at the same time.

"Yeah. She's pretty."

Meg stole a quick look at David out of the corner of her eye. A question leapt to her lips but it was so unusual and irregular, she kept quiet. For the first time in her life, she was wondering whether David thought she was pretty.

She frowned, crossed her arms, and mulled it over. David was much too short to be her boyfriend. But who knew what the future might bring? If he ate enough, he was sure to grow taller.

"How 'bout a sandwich?" Meg asked.

David sat up straight at the mention of food. "I gotta move my bike first." He stood up, brushing bits of leaves and dust from the back of his jeans. "I just sort of left it out front here because I was in a hurry."

"Oh, forget that. Leave it there, David," Meg said quickly. "If my friends ask, I'll just tell 'em you're my sidekick, okay?"

"How about your mentor?" David asked.

"I don't know what that means."

"It means I'm smarter than you are." David grinned broadly.

"Then we'll have to think of something else," Meg said as they walked into the house together.

About the Author

MARY LOCKE, born in Schenectady, New York, spent most of her childhood in Bloomington, Illinois. Locke's unending curiosity in the government has been the basis for much of her work experience both in the United States and abroad. From reporting on town governments and elections for the *Framingham News* in Massachusetts, to serving as a liaison between the U.S. and foreign embassies in East Asia, Ms. Locke has seen a considerable amount of goings-on in government activities.

Her first novel, *The Summer the Spies Moved In*, reflects a comical side of Ms. Locke's intrigue in government affairs. She currently lives in London with her husband, two children, and a hamster.

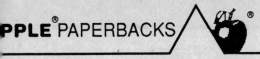